A SILENCED WOMAN

SURYA VENKATESH

Made with ♥ on the Notion Press Platform
www.notionpress.com

This novel is lovingly dedicated to my mother, **Kala.**

Love you, AMMA.

Contents

Contents

FOREWORD

In a world where the voices of women have often been stifled, where their stories have remained untold, and where their struggles have been ignored, "A Silenced Woman" emerges as a powerful testament to their resilience, strength, and courage. This novel is not just a story; it is a tribute to the countless women who have fought to reclaim their voices, their rights, and their dignity. It is a reflection of the challenges women face, the battles they fight daily, and the unwavering spirit that enables them to rise, no matter how deep the scars.

As you journey through the pages of this book, you will find yourself immersed in the emotional turmoil, the heartache, and the triumphs of its characters. The story unfolds with raw honesty, depicting the pain of silencing, the struggle to be heard, and the relentless pursuit of justice. But it is also a story of hope—a story that shows us that even in the darkest of times, the light of resilience can pierce through the shadows.

This novel is born from the experiences of the women around me—those who have lived through hardships, faced unspeakable challenges, and yet continue to inspire. Their strength is woven into every word, every scene, and every character. This is a story that belongs to them. It belongs to every woman who has been told she is not enough, whose dreams have been crushed, but who continues to fight for her place in the world.

But it is also a story that speaks to all of us. It calls on us to examine the world we live in, the systems that perpetuate inequality, and the ways in which we can all contribute to a more just and compassionate society. It calls on us to listen—to truly listen—to the voices that have long been silenced.

As you read "A Silenced Woman," I invite you to reflect on the power of your own voice. Know that it has the ability to shape the world around you, to change lives, and to uplift those who are struggling to be heard. In the pages of this book, you will find the courage to stand up, to speak out, and to be a part of the movement that will create a world where women's voices are no longer silenced.

Thank you for picking up this book. Your choice is an act of solidarity with every woman who has ever been silenced. It is my hope that, as you turn each page, you will be reminded of the power of storytelling, the importance of resilience, and the unyielding spirit of women everywhere.

With gratitude and hope,

Surya Venkatesh

Preface

The journey of writing "A Silenced Woman" has been both deeply personal and profoundly reflective of the world we live in today. This book is not just a work of fiction; it is an exploration of the inner strength and resilience of women, woven together with the struggles, silences, and triumphs that many have experienced, yet so often go unspoken.

The idea for this story was born from the stories I've heard, the experiences I've witnessed, and the emotions I've shared with the incredible women in my life—my mother, my sisters, my friends, my colleagues, and even the women whose voices have been lost in the noise of everyday life. These women, with their dreams, hopes, and the unyielding strength they carry in the face of unimaginable adversity, have been the true inspiration behind this book.

This novel explores the profound pain of being silenced—not just through the words that go unspoken, but through the very actions of society that often seek to suppress women's voices, dreams, and ambitions. It is about the way women are often expected to shrink themselves, to take a backseat to others, to remain unseen or unheard, despite their power, wisdom, and ability to change the world around them.

The story you are about to read is one of courage, resilience, and the determination to rise above the forces that seek to hold us down. It is about breaking free from the confines of silence and stepping into the light of one's truth, however difficult that may be. It is about the power of reclaiming your voice—no matter how long it takes—and the ripple effect it has, not only in your own life, but in the lives of those around you.

I write this not only for the women who have experienced these struggles but for everyone who believes in the power of equality, justice, and the need to stand up for what is right. While the events within the pages of this book may be fictional, the emotions, the heartache, and the ultimate strength that comes from overcoming oppression are very real. These are the stories of women across the world, and they deserve to be heard, to be honored, and to be celebrated.

This book is a dedication to all those who have been silenced, whether by society, circumstance, or their own fears. It is a tribute to those who, despite the odds, continue to fight for their place in the world and to speak their truth, no matter the cost.

I hope that as you read "A Silenced Woman," you will not just see the story of one character, but the story of many. You will see the lives of women who have been stifled, but whose resilience and strength refuse to be suppressed. And through their voices, may we all find the courage to rise, to speak, and to make the world hear us.

Thank you for joining me on this journey.

ACKNOWLEDGEMENTS

A Heartfelt Tribute

With deepest reverence, I bow to my Lord, Shiva, whose divine guidance not only illuminates my path but also inspires the very depths of my soul. In moments of uncertainty, it is His wisdom that provides clarity and strength, reminding me of the power of faith and devotion.

To my incredible family, who have been my unwavering rock throughout this journey, I extend my heartfelt gratitude. Your love and support have been the bedrock of my achievements, and I am eternally thankful for the sacrifices you have made for my growth.

To my beloved mother, Kala and my brother, Paramesh your unwavering support and unconditional love from the foundation upon which I build my dreams. Your belief in me has always served as a beacon of light, guiding me through challenges and triumphs alike.

To my Cherished cousins, Manoj, Padma Vadina and Nagendra, as well as my dear uncle Prasad, your encouragement and guidance have been invaluable. You have stood by me as pillars of strength. I am honored to have you as part of my life.

To my dear nephew and niece, Karthika and Nihal, your innocent smiles and joyful laughter are my ultimate stress busters. In your presence, I am reminded of life's simple pleasures, the beauty of innocence, and the joy of living in the moment.

To my dear friend, Harini, your complete faith in me and this book means the world to me. Your thoughtful reading and endless support have been a source of inspiration and motivation, pushing me to delve deeper into my craft. I am grateful for our friendship, which adds richness to my journey.

Thanks to all the women who have fought for their voices to be heard, who have broken the chains of silence, and who continue to inspire the world with their strength, courage, and resilience. Your stories are the foundation of this book, and it is through your unwavering spirit that the world will change.

And to you, my dear reader, thank you for embracing this story and becoming an essential part of my journey. Your trust, curiosity, and enthusiasm fuel my passion for writing. It is your engagement that transforms my solitary endeavor into a shared experience, and for that, I am forever grateful.

With love, gratitude, and blessings,

Surya Venkatesh

Prologue

The evening had brought an unusual stillness, broken only by the occasional rustle of leaves outside the modest home perched on the hills. It was meant to be a time of recovery—a refuge from the chaos of the world. Satya Sree had withdrawn from her thriving movement, seeking a moment to lay down her burdens, evade the relentless voices and battles, and simply exist as herself.

But peace is short-lived when the past refuses to stay buried.

Heavy footsteps crunching gravel broke the silence. At first, the sound was faint, barely noticeable. Then it grew louder, nearer, deliberate. Satya's heart raced. She looked at her, whose innocent eyes met hers with a mix of curiosity and unease.

The knock at the door was not a plea but a command. When the door swung open, the sight before Satya froze her in place. A man stood there, fury in his eyes, flanked by two men radiating dark intent. The past she had worked so hard to escape was at her doorstep, demanding a price she wasn't sure she could pay.

In an instant, the serene evening spiraled into chaos. The walls of the house bore witness to violence and desperation, the air heavy with fear and resolve. At that moment, Satya realized her battles were far from over—and this time, the stakes were greater than ever.

This is the story of Satya, a woman who dared to raise her voice when others remained silent. A woman who sacrificed everything to empower the voiceless, only to confront the one battle she had always dreaded: the fight to protect her family.

Her journey will plunge into the depths of despair and soar to the heights of resilience. As past and present collide, one question remains: How far will a silenced woman go to protect the ones she loves?

I

A façade

"Oh, you're so lucky!" one aunt exclaimed, adjusting a flower in her hair. "A boy like him—who wouldn't want this match?"

It was my engagement day. I felt as if I was floating through someone else's life, out of place in my own world. I had just taken a bath, and as I stepped back into my room, a crowd of aunts and cousins were already waiting, eyes gleaming with excitement. They fussed around me, transforming me into the perfect bride-to-be, their voices overlapping in a whirlwind of cheerful chatter.

The talk quickly turned to the groom-to-be. A software engineer, well-established and making a solid income—lakhs a month. His family was known for their wealth and elegance, rooted in all the comforts she'd only dreamed of. The women brought out makeup kits and jewelry, draping me in a rich, glittering saree. I looked at every part of the bride, I felt more like a doll—one being dressed and decorated without a say in her own story.

I tried to let myself feel the excitement buzzing around me. After all, I thought, he seemed kind, gentle. My parents had all but insisted that this was the right choice for me, reminding me repeatedly of how good a match he was.

But even as they applied the finishing touches to my look, my mind drifted. I remembered that first meeting with him—the pelli chupulu, the day my family had formally introduced me to my future husband. I hadn't known then what to feel; everything had been a blur of expectations, a mixture of happiness and confusion.

Flashback to Pelli Chupulu Day

That day, the house was a whirlwind of activity, with my mother at the center of it all, her excitement palpable as she prepared for the arrival of the boy's family. She knew they were wealthy, and it was clear she had been praying fervently, hoping they would find me suitable. My father, in contrast, remained calm, appearing indifferent to the commotion. Yet, as their only daughter, I felt the weight of their expectations settling heavily upon me.

When I caught a glimpse of myself in the mirror, the reflection startled me. Draped in an elegant saree with my hair neatly braided, I looked transformed—like an angel, adorned with layers of makeup and jewelry. My mother, overwhelmed, approached, kissed my cheek, and whispered, "You look beautiful." Her excitement was contagious, even though a part of me felt uneasy.

"Just stay calm, smile, and don't reveal too much," she instructed, her expression serious. "If the boy wants to talk to you privately, just share your likes—don't delve into your past. Let them see the present version of you."

"What is this, Ma?" I retorted, frustrated. "If he's going to marry me, shouldn't he know everything about me? Why should I hide anything? I'm educated; I know what I want and

how to speak for myself."

"Silence, Just listen to me and stop arguing," she replied sharply.

We were still bickering when the sound of a car pulling into the driveway reached us. My heart pounded as I rushed to my room, closing the door softly. My mother hurried to the kitchen, while my father, uncle, and cousins went to welcome the guests.

Peeking out of the window, I saw them step out of the car: two women, likely his mother and sister, and an older man—his father, I presumed. Then, he emerged. My would-be groom was tall and well-built, dressed impeccably in a crisp formal shirt. His demeanor was polished, his smile calm and polite. Although his complexion was average, there was an understated charm about him.

A strange thought crossed my mind: If everything went well, this man could become my husband. How surreal, I mused, that a single meeting might determine a lifelong partnership. How could anyone decide something so significant in just an hour?

I found it ironic. My family had always discouraged interactions with boys, yet here I was, expected to make a monumental decision in minutes. What if he didn't share my views or interests? What if marriage revealed a character mismatch?

As these thoughts raced through my mind, a gentle nudge on my shoulder startled me. Turning around, I saw my friend Maggi grinning. "Lost in thought, are we?" she teased.

The pelli chupulu was a blur. I exchanged only a few polite words with him. He seemed nice but distant—formal in a way that felt uncomfortable. Still, I smiled and tried to appear cheerful, playing the role of the eager bride-to-be.

Now, alone in my room, doubt crept in. Was this truly what I wanted? Was this the life I had envisioned? I had always dreamed of love—of finding someone who understood, challenged, and inspired me. But this felt more like a transaction than a love story.

A knock on the door. Maggi entered, her expression sympathetic. "You okay?" she asked, sitting beside me.

"It was all a blur, Maggi," I sighed, my gaze drifting to the window. "We barely spoke. Just polite nods and forced smiles. He seemed nice, but there was this... distance. Like we were strangers performing a script."

Maggi, ever empathetic, reached out and squeezed my hand. "It's a lot to process, isn't it? Deciding your future in just a few hours."

"I keep thinking about what I really want," I whispered. "I've always dreamed of a love story—someone who truly understands me. But this... this feels like a compromise. I am silenced."

A heavy silence followed. Maggi understood the gravity of my words. "You don't have to go through with this, you know. Your happiness matters more than anyone else's expectations."

A wave of doubt washed over me. "But what about my parents? They've sacrificed so much for me."

"They love you, and they want you to be happy," Maggi reassured me. "They'll understand, even if it means breaking tradition."

I thought of my parents and their dreams for me. They had given up so much, and I didn't want to disappoint them. But I couldn't ignore my own feelings and aspirations.

As I reflected on Maggi's words, a bittersweet smile crossed my lips. I knew I had a difficult decision to make—one that would shape my life.

That night, lying in bed, I couldn't sleep. The weight of my decision pressed heavily on me. I thought about my dreams and aspirations. Had I truly abandoned them, or was there still hope?

As the first light of dawn seeped through the curtains, I made a choice. I wouldn't let others dictate my life. I would fight for my happiness, no matter the cost.

ഇ

The sound of the aunt's shout pulled me back to the present. My heart pounded with a mixture of excitement and dread. Today was the day. The day I would become engaged to a man I barely knew. A man chosen for me, not by me.

I took a deep breath, trying to calm my racing thoughts. I had tried to voice my concerns to my parents, but they had dismissed them, assuring me that this was the best decision for me. They had painted a picture of a perfect future, a life of comfort and security. But I couldn't shake the feeling that I was sacrificing my own dreams and desires for their expectations.

As I descended the stairs, I caught a glimpse of my reflection in the mirror. The once-familiar face staring back at me was now adorned with heavy makeup and traditional jewelry. I felt like a stranger in my own skin, a puppet controlled by societal norms and family pressure.

The ceremony was full of rituals and blessings. I exchanged rings with my fiancé, a mechanical smile plastered on my face. The guests showered us with compliments and well wishes, their voices mingling with the celebratory music. But amidst the festivities, I felt a growing sense of isolation.

As the engagement ceremony drew to a close, I couldn't shake the feeling that I was living a lie. The smile plastered on my face felt forced, the laughter around me seemed hollow. Everyone else celebrated, yet I felt an unbearable weight pressing down on me, making it hard to breathe. Vittal, my fiancé, stood beside me, his hand warm around mine, but I couldn't help but wonder if he felt the same sense of entrapment. Was he genuinely happy in this arranged marriage, or was he merely playing his part?

As we posed for photos, I caught Maggi's eye across the room. Her sympathetic smile was a lifeline in my sea of confusion; she understood my turmoil without me having to say a word. The day passed in a haze of relatives and friends offering gifts and good wishes, my parents beaming with pride. Their happiness only deepened my sense of isolation.

Once the last guest departed and the house fell silent, I locked myself in my room. I let out a deep sigh as I collapsed onto the bed, the weight of my doubts crushing me. I thought about Vittal and the life we were supposed to build together. Would we truly be happy? Would we find common ground, or would we end up as strangers cohabitating out of obligation?

The questions swirled in my mind like a relentless vortex, pulling me under. I knew I couldn't keep quiet forever; I needed someone to confide in—someone who wouldn't judge me. I reached for my phone and dialed Maggi's number.

"Hey," she answered on the first ring, her voice a comforting anchor.

"How are you holding up?" she asked.

"I don't know, Maggi," I whispered, my voice trembling. "I feel like I'm losing myself in all this. I don't know if I can go through with it."

Maggi's voice was calm and reassuring. "You don't have to make any decisions tonight. Just take things one step at a time. But promise me one thing: talk to Vittal. Really talk to him. Ask him about his dreams, his aspirations. See if you can connect on a deeper level."

I nodded, even though she couldn't see me. "I'll try."

As I hung up the phone, a flicker of hope ignited within me. Maybe, just maybe, I could find a way to make this work. Perhaps I could learn to love Vittal, to build a life with him that was more than just a façade. But as I lay in bed, staring at the ceiling, I knew the path wouldn't be easy.

II

Reaching Out

The darkness of night had masked my doubts, but morning's clarity brought them into sharp focus. As I stood at the crossroads, the weight of expectation threatened to suffocate me. I knew I had to take a leap of faith, to shatter the chains of destiny that bound me to a life I hadn't chosen. But how could I silence the voices of tradition, family, and fear, and find the courage to forge my own path?

I couldn't shake the feeling that I was trapped in a gilded cage, a prisoner of societal expectations. I needed to connect with Vittal on a deeper level, to see if there was a spark, a genuine connection beyond the superficial pleasantries.But the problem was, I didn't have his contact information. My mother had kept it from me, probably fearing I'd repeat the "nonsense" I pulled last time—where I'd found the previous suitor's number and called him, only to realize our personalities clashed horribly, leading to a canceled match. This time, she was extra careful, leaving me with no way to reach Vittal.

Determined, I searched for any clues. I grabbed my dad's phone first, scrolling through his contacts, but there was nothing under "Vittal." I switched to my mom's phone, my hands shaking slightly. I searched every possible contact name but again, nothing. Finally, I opened Instagram, typing "Vittal Krishna" in the search bar, hoping he'd be among the profiles that appeared.

After scrolling for what felt like an eternity, I found his profile. His picture was unmistakable—Vittal, smiling warmly, his eyes framed by stylish sunglasses. I felt a little thrill as I sent him a friend request, wondering if he'd recognize my profile. Minutes passed, then an hour, each one dragging as I waited for the notification that he'd accepted.

Four hours later, it finally came. I quickly opened his profile, and his new profile picture appeared—still him, now with a broader smile, looking relaxed. I was relieved to feel a little connection, like I was finally breaking through the invisible barrier between us.

Without hesitating, I typed, "Hi." My heart pounded as I waited for his response, which came faster than I expected.

"Hello, Satya Sree," he replied, followed by another message. "It's amazing to see your message."

He seemed genuinely pleased, and his enthusiasm surprised me. What should I say next? I wondered, quickly typing, "Yes, I felt like talking with you."

"That's great! Even I felt the same," he replied almost instantly.

There was a pause as I tried to gather the courage to ask for his number. I knew I had to know him beyond this one-dimensional text conversation if we were going to move forward together.

"Hope you don't mind sharing your number?" I asked, feeling a nervous flutter in my stomach as I hit send.

Seconds later, his reply popped up: "Of course, I'd love to talk properly. Here's my number: 98765xxxxxx."

As I saved his contact, I felt a cautious optimism. This was my chance to get to know him, to see if we could find real compatibility and make this marriage more than just a facade. I couldn't help but feel a surge of excitement. This was the beginning of a new chapter, a chance to write my own destiny.I couldn't wait to talk to him, to really get to know him. But at the same time, a wave of doubt washed over me. Was I ready to share my true self with him?

With trembling fingers, I opened WhatsApp and sent him a message: "What's the good time to talk with you?"

"Right now I am in the office, Can we talk in the evening?" he replied promptly.

Relief washed over me. He was interested! I quickly typed out a reply: "Sure, once you reach home, please ping me."

As I waited for his response, my heart pounded in my chest. Every passing minute felt like an eternity. I couldn't help but check my phone incessantly, hoping for a notification.

I shared my excitement with Maggi, who was thrilled that I had taken the initiative. She showered me with advice, from what to talk about to how to behave. While I appreciated her enthusiasm, I couldn't shake the feeling that I was walking a tightrope.

As the hours passed, I couldn't help but wonder if I should reveal my past to Vittal. A part of me wanted to be completely honest with him, but another part feared the consequences. If my mother found out, she would be furious. I couldn't imagine the storm that would ensue.

I decided to take a cautious approach. I would wait and see how our conversations unfolded. If the right moment presented itself, I would share my story. But for now, I would focus on building a genuine connection with Vittal, one step at a time.

The evening finally arrived, bringing with it a wave of anticipation mingled with nerves. I paced back and forth in my room, glancing at my phone every few seconds, my heart racing with the prospect of what was to come. Finally, a notification lit up my screen: a message from Vittal.

"Hi, I'm free now. Can we talk?"

I took a deep breath, steadying myself for the moment. This is it, I thought, and quickly replied, "Sure, call me."

Moments later, my phone rang, and with a surge of courage, I answered.

"Hi," his voice was calm and warm, immediately putting me at ease. "How are you?"

"I'm good," I replied, my voice surprisingly steady despite the butterflies in my stomach. "How about you?"

"Doing well, thanks. It's nice to finally talk with you." There was a friendliness in his tone that felt like a warm embrace.

"Yeah, same here," I said, a smile spreading across my face as I sank into the comfort of our conversation. "So, what's new with you?"

"Oh, you know, just work. The usual routine," he chuckled. "How about you? What do you do to keep busy?"

I laughed nervously, my mind racing for something interesting to share. "Oh, not much, just reading a lot lately."

"Oh, really? What are you reading?" he asked, his genuine curiosity making me feel at ease.

I froze for a split second, panic creeping in. Quick, think of a book! "Uh... I'm reading *Three mistakes in my life.* It's a classic," I said, hoping I sounded convincing.

"Nice choice! I've read that a couple of times. It's a fantastic book," he replied, and a wave of relief washed over me. But then I worried—what if he asked more about it? Frantically, I recalled a few details I'd read online and tried to sound casual. "Oh, I know, right? I love the characters."

After a comfortable pause, he broke the silence. "Hey, I was thinking... It's surprising that we haven't had a chance to really talk since our first meeting and even during our engagement. Maybe we could meet up sometime? Just for coffee or something casual? It would be nice to chat freely."

My heart raced at the invitation. He seemed genuinely interested in getting to know me better.

"Yeah, sure, that sounds good," I replied, striving to keep my tone light. "There's a new café near Madhapur. We could meet there?"

"Perfect! How about this weekend?" he suggested, and I felt a rush of excitement.

"That works for me," I replied, barely able to contain my glee.

We chatted a bit longer, the conversation flowing effortlessly, both of us sensing the budding connection between us. I could feel a smile spreading across my face as we exchanged our goodbyes. Setting my phone down a soft smile still on my face.

III

First Impressions

Two days later, I stepped into the Icon café near Madhapur, my heart pounding in my chest as the warm glow of pendant lights cast flickering shadows around the room. The soft hum of jazz filled the air, but it felt distant, almost drowned out by the rush of adrenaline coursing through me. My eyes darted across the room, searching frantically until I spotted him—Vittal, looking effortlessly stylish in a crisp white shirt, his hand raised in a casual wave from a corner table, drawing me in like a moth to a flame.

"Hey, you look lovely," he said, standing up to greet me with a warm smile.

"Thanks, you too," I replied, feeling a blush rise to my cheeks. His presence was calm, but somehow electrifying.

We settled in, ordered our coffee, and began chatting. The conversation flowed easily, as if we were old friends reconnecting. We covered everything from our favorite books (I made sure to avoid *the book Three mistakes in my life* this time) to childhood memories that had us both laughing.

He shared stories of summer vacations spent at his grandparents' village, of days filled with mango-picking and chasing fireflies. I told him about my own childhood mischiefs—the time I'd tried to "adopt" a stray dog and hid it in my room, only to get caught by my mother. Each story brought a new round of laughter, breaking down any lingering nerves.

As we chatted, I felt a strange sense of ease settle over me. The way he listened, with genuine interest, made me feel like he truly saw me, not the careful image I often showed to the world. It was comforting and a little disarming.

After a comfortable silence, he leaned back, looking at me thoughtfully. "You know, it's nice being able to talk like this. Sometimes, with people, it feels like you're playing a role. But with you, it just feels... natural."

I nodded, knowing exactly what he meant. "Yeah, it feels the same for me. I guess some connections just... flow."

A gentle smile spread across his face. We continued talking, sharing pieces of ourselves, both careful and yet curious. And as the evening wore on, I couldn't shake the feeling that, for the first time in a long time, I was exactly where I needed to be.

After coffee, Vittal suggested a walk by the nearby Durgam Cheruvu lake. The evening air was filled with the sweet scent of blooming flowers.

"I'm glad we're doing this," he said, turning to me as we strolled. "I feel like I've gotten to know you better in this meeting."

"I know, exactly what you mean," I replied, smiling.

As the sun dipped below the horizon, casting a golden glow across the lake, Vittal took my hand. It felt like a spark of electricity had passed between us.

"May I ask you something?" he said, his eyes locked on mine.

"Of course," I replied, my heart racing.

"Do you believe in arranged marriages?" he asked, his voice low and thoughtful.

I hesitated, unsure of how to respond.The question lingered in the air between us, and I felt a slight tension settle around us as I searched for the right words.

"Honestly," I began, my voice barely above a whisper, "I'm still figuring that out myself. Arranged marriages... They make sense in so many ways. The support from family, the shared values... but it's also scary, the idea of committing to someone you don't really know." I glanced down, gathering my thoughts. "I guess I always dreamed of choosing someone for myself, but I also know how important my family's happiness is to me."

He nodded, his expression thoughtful. "I get that. My family feels the same way, and I respect their views. But a part of me hopes to find a deeper connection, someone who I feel drawn to in a way that goes beyond just compatibility on paper."

I smiled, relieved that he understood. "It sounds like we're on the same page."

We continued our walk in comfortable silence, the distant hum of city lights blending with the soft sounds of the Durgam cheruvu lake. I felt a sense of peace I hadn't felt in a long time. Vittal wasn't just any person arranged by my family; he was someone who shared my hopes, my fears. And that realization made everything feel... possible.

"Satya," he said after a moment, breaking the silence, "Would it be alright if we took things slow? To really get to know each other before making any big decisions?"

I felt a wave of relief wash over me. "Yes, I'd like that," I said, smiling. "It's important to me, too."

As we walked, hand in hand, Vittal's expression turned contemplative. His grip tightened slightly, drawing my attention.

"May I share something with you?" he asked, his voice laced with vulnerability.

"Of course," I replied, sensing a depth to his words that went beyond the surface of our arranged engagement.

Vittal took a deep breath, his gaze drifting towards the lake.

"I was in a serious relationship a few years ago. Her name was Latha. We were together for five years, and I thought we'd spend our lives together," he confessed, his voice filled with a hint of melancholy.

"What happened?" I asked gently, my heart aching for him.

"We wanted different things. She wanted to settle abroad, while I wanted to stay in India. We tried to make it work, but...it fell apart," he admitted, his voice wavering.

"I was devastated. I thought I'd lost my soulmate. The breakup was messy, and it took a long time to heal." His eyes clouded over, lost in a sea of painful memories.

"I'm so sorry," I whispered, squeezing his hand gently.

He looked at me, his eyes searching for understanding.

"You know, it's funny. Everyone expects me to be this strong, successful guy, but inside, I'm still healing. Still trying to make sense of it all," he confessed, his voice breaking slightly.

I listened intently, my heart aching for him. In that moment, I saw the pain, the vulnerability, and the sincerity in his eyes.

"You're not alone," I said softly, reaching out to brush away a stray tear.

Vittal's gaze locked onto mine, and I saw a glimmer of hope.

"Thank you for listening," he whispered, his voice filled with gratitude.

As the stars twinkled brighter above, our hands intertwined, I knew that our connection had deepened, transcending the boundaries of our arranged engagement.The evening breeze carried the soft lapping of water against the shore as Vittal and I strolled along the lake. The sky was a canvas of twilight hues, and the stars began to twinkle, casting a magical glow over the serene landscape.

As Vittal's eyes searched mine, emotions stirred within me. His openness, the way he'd revealed his own pain, touched something deep inside. I could feel his unspoken invitation to reciprocate, to share my own past in return.

My thoughts drifted to memories I hadn't revisited in a long time—memories of my ex-boyfriend, of stolen moments and promises that once meant the world to me. Happiness and heartache intertwined, lingering like a bittersweet fragrance I couldn't shake. But then, my mother's voice echoed in my mind, a warning as familiar as it was firm: "Boys can share their past, but girls shouldn't. They'll judge you, Satyasree. Always keep your secrets safe."

I felt a pang of hesitation, fear pulling me back even as a small part of me longed to open up to Vittal. Was I ready to take that risk? To trust him, to let him see the parts of me that I'd hidden for so long?

Vittal seemed to sense my inner struggle, his gaze softening as he quietly asked, "What's on your mind, Satya?"

I swallowed, my words caught in a delicate balance between honesty and self-preservation. "Nothing... just... I'm still processing everything," I replied, trying to keep my tone casual, but feeling the weight of the truth I hadn't shared.

For a moment, he simply held my gaze, as if seeing through the layers I'd wrapped around myself. But he didn't press. Instead, he nodded, accepting my answer even if he knew there was more. It was as if he understood my reluctance and respected it, giving me the space to reveal myself on my own terms.

As we strolled by the lake, a thousand thoughts swirled through my mind, each one louder than the last.

Should I share my past with Vittal? Would he understand, or would he see me differently? Mom's warning echoed, her words urging caution, reminding me of the judgment that might follow if I revealed too much. Yet, Vittal's openness had made me question her advice. His honesty felt like an invitation, like a hand outstretched, urging me to trust him.

What if sharing my story brought us closer together? What if he could accept my past as simply a part of who I am? But just as quickly, a shadow of doubt surfaced. What if my truth shattered what we were building?

I was caught in a vortex of uncertainty, torn between fear and hope. Each question felt heavier than the last, each answer more elusive.

As the stars emerged, their light reflecting in the lake's rippling surface, I made a quiet promise to myself: I'll share my story with Vittal, but on my own terms. I'll wait until I'm ready, until I find the courage to bare that part of myself. And when that time comes, if our connection is as real as I feel it is, maybe it will survive the truth.

For now, though, I would keep my secrets safe. Vittal's hand still held mine, his fingers entwined with a gentle strength, grounding me. In that touch, I found a flicker of reassurance—one that reminded me that, for this moment, I didn't have to reveal everything. And yet, as his thumb brushed lightly over mine, I wondered: would our bond be strong enough to hold steady when the truth finally came to light?

We lingered by the lake a little longer, both of us absorbing this new, quiet understanding. As the sky darkened, we walked back to the café, talking and laughing easily, each step feeling lighter than the last. This might not be the love story I'd once dreamed of, but maybe, just maybe, it could be the start of something beautiful.

IV

Shadows

Days turned into weeks, and what started as tentative steps toward connection blossomed into something deep and unbreakable. Vittal and I became inseparable, sharing every detail of our lives with an ease that felt almost unreal. Our conversations flowed like a gentle stream, each topic blending seamlessly into the next. We lost track of time in these conversations, as though the world had shrunk to just the two of us.

We discovered shared passions that bound us even closer—our mutual love for old Telugu movies, the kind with soulful songs and grand storytelling, and a shared longing to explore the world, one hiking trail at a time. The miles between us seemed to vanish as our laughter filled our calls, and even our silences became a language of their own, carrying the comfort of simply being present.

Our parents, noticing the depth of our bond, soon took the next step. One evening, my mom approached me, her eyes bright with excitement. "Satya, we've fixed a date for the marriage," she announced, her voice filled with warmth.

My heart skipped as I looked over at Vittal, who was already watching me with a knowing smile. In that moment, our excitement was like an unspoken promise, filling the space between us. This was it—the beginning of our future together.

Vittal and I joined forces for wedding shopping, and our laughter filled the air as we navigated the crowded markets together. We sifted through endless aisles of colors, fabrics, and jewelry, weaving memories into every choice we made. For the ceremony, I selected a stunning saree that made me feel both nervous and beautiful, while Vittal chose a classic, elegant kurta. Our smiles mirrored each other's excitement, reflecting the anticipation we both felt.

Yet beneath the surface of joy, I could sense an undercurrent of tension that weighed on my heart. Vittal's parents, particularly his father, seemed increasingly fixated on dowry, an uncomfortable reminder of the expectations placed upon my family. "We expect a substantial amount, considering our family's status," his father stated one evening, his voice laced with an unwavering firmness that left no room for negotiation.

My parents, though already financially stretched, bore the burden silently. To meet the demands, they made sacrifices I could scarcely bear to imagine—they sold pieces of our ancestral jewelry, family heirlooms that had been passed down for generations, and took on loans that would weigh on them for years.

"Satya, don't worry about the expenses," Mom whispered to me one night, her voice gentle but weary. "Your happiness is all that matters to us."

Her words filled me with both love and a pang of guilt, knowing the sacrifices they made for my future. A wave of doubt crept in, mingling with my excitement—could this marriage, despite all the love between Vittal and me, be truly free of these shadows?

As wedding preparations continued, the contrast between our families' values grew painfully clear. Vittal's parents seemed fixated on material wealth and status, while my parents cherished love, respect, and the simple joy of bringing two families together. I couldn't ignore the discomfort building inside me.

One evening, as Vittal and I walked along a quiet path, I finally gathered the courage to ask, "Vittal, do you believe in dowry?" My voice was laced with concern, hoping he understood the weight of my question.

He paused, his gaze steady but thoughtful, and then spoke firmly. "No, Satya. I don't believe in it. Love can't be measured in money or gifts. But at the same time, I feel a responsibility to respect my parents' beliefs, even if I don't fully share them."

A silence fell between us, one that wasn't uncomfortable but filled with an unspoken understanding. His words were reassuring, yet I sensed the complexity of the situation—that delicate balance between honoring his love for me and his loyalty to his family's values.

In that moment, I realized that, despite the love we shared, our journey would demand patience, resilience, and a strength that came not just from us but from the choices we'd each have to make.

As our marriage ceremony drew near, excitement buzzed around us, yet I couldn't shake a growing sense of unease. There was a quiet tension in Vittal, a hint of something unresolved, and it gnawed at me, even as we went about our preparations.

One evening, while we were out selecting the final pieces for our ceremony attire, Vittal's phone rang. He glanced at the screen, his expression tightening before he answered. "Hey, Prashanth," he said softly, his voice barely above a whisper. His posture shifted, and he turned away slightly, as if shielding me from the conversation.

The few words he muttered were low and cryptic, but his tense brow and the way his smile vanished made it clear that something was weighing on him.

When he hung up, I couldn't help but ask, "Everything okay?"

He forced a reassuring smile, dismissing it. "It's nothing, Satya. Just an old friend from college."

But his words felt hollow, and in his usually bright eyes, there was a clouded depth I hadn't seen before. That night, as we sat under a canopy of stars on the rooftop, I decided to press a little further.

"Vittal," I began gently, "if something's on your mind, you can tell me. I'm here for you."

He took a long, steadying breath, his gaze lifting to the night sky as if seeking courage from the stars. "Satya, there's something I haven't told you. Something that could change everything between us."

My heart skipped, and I reached out, my hand resting on his. "Whatever it is, just tell me," I whispered, trying to keep the tremor from my voice.

He met my eyes, a mix of fear and vulnerability reflecting in his own. "I promise, I'll tell you soon. But right now... I just need to know you're here with me."

In that moment, a silent understanding passed between us, one deeper than words could express. I wrapped my fingers around his, giving a gentle squeeze. "Whatever it is, we'll face it together," I vowed.

As we sat there, an unspoken promise anchored us. But in the back of my mind, a lingering worry grew, knowing that secrets, however well-intended, could test even the strongest of bonds.

My gaze drifted to Vittal's phone as one message flashed on the screen which Vittal has typed: "Madhu, I'll always keep my promise."

My heart skipped a beat, a wave of unease washing over me. Who was Madhu? And what promise had Vittal made to her?

I took a steadying breath, trying to keep my voice casual. "Vittal... who's Madhu?"

He tensed, and I watched as a flicker of panic crossed his face. His eyes darted away, avoiding my own. "No one, Satya," he said, too quickly. "Just an old friend."

But his words lacked their usual warmth and confidence, and the uneasy feeling only grew. A crack had appeared in our trust, small yet unmistakable, and I couldn't shake the chill creeping into my heart.

As silence stretched between us, doubt settled in. Was there a side of Vittal I didn't know? And how deep did this hidden past run?

Despite his assurances, the questions began to build. Was this "promise" to Madhu a relic of his past, or was it something more? And as much as I wanted to believe him, I couldn't ignore the nagging feeling that something significant—and possibly painful—was lying in the shadows of our relationship.

As we sat there, words unsaid, I found myself questioning the man I was about to marry. Could I ignore this doubt? Or was this the start of something that would force us to confront truths neither of us were prepared for?

ജ

Days drifted by, but I couldn't shake the haunting echo of Vittal's message to Madhu. Who was she? What promise had he made? Every conversation with him now felt strained, as if an invisible wall had risen between us.

Finally, I confided in Maggi, hoping she might offer some clarity. "Maggi, I'm worried," I began, my voice barely a whisper.

Her brow furrowed with concern. "What's wrong?"

I took a deep breath, the words feeling heavy. "Vittal's been... different. He got a call from someone named Madhu, and when I asked, he brushed it off, saying she was just an old friend. But I can't shake the feeling he's hiding something."

Maggi's expression turned serious. "Do you trust him?"

The question lingered, weighted and uncomfortable. "I want to," I said softly. "But what if there's more to this? What if he's hiding something from me?"

Maggi's gaze softened, her voice gentle but firm. "Satya, you owe it to yourself to find out. Talk to him. Clear the air before you make any decisions."

But fear held me back. What if uncovering the truth revealed cracks I couldn't ignore? The doubts clawed at me, making me question if the life I'd imagined with Vittal was as solid as I believed—or if it was built on something fragile, something that might shatter at the slightest touch.

That night, as I lay awake, I realized I couldn't avoid this conversation forever. The truth, no matter how painful, was better than living with uncertainty. But could I find the courage to ask him? And if I did, would I be ready for whatever answer he might give?

As wedding preparations intensified, the unease within me grew. Every detail seemed to spotlight the widening gap between our families' values. For my parents, the marriage was about joy and unity; for Vittal's, it felt like an endless checklist of status symbols and demands.

൨

One evening, while choosing flowers for the ceremony, Vittal's mother mentioned Madhu in passing. "Oh, and Vittal's friend Madhu will be attending. She wouldn't miss it for the world," she said, barely glancing up.

My heart raced. Who was this Madhu? A casual mention, yet the name held a weight that seemed to press on my chest.

Vittal noticed my expression change. "Satya, is everything okay?"

I forced a smile. "Yes, just tired," I lied, trying to bury the creeping doubt. But a seed had been planted, and it was growing, twisting my heart in knots.

That night, we found a quiet moment together. The stars blinked above, and I knew I couldn't carry this alone any longer. I had to ask.

"Vittal," I began, my voice trembling slightly, "can we talk?"

He turned to me, his eyes gentle but questioning. "Of course, Satya. You can tell me anything."

I took a deep breath, steadying myself. "Who is Madhu? Really?"

His face shifted, surprise flickering in his eyes. There was a pause, heavy and charged, before he answered.

"She's...someone from my past. We were close once, and she's remained a friend. But that's all," he said, his voice calm but distant.

His answer was simple, yet it did little to soothe my worry. "Why didn't you tell me about her before?" I pressed, my voice softer, almost pleading.

Vittal sighed, looking away. “I didn’t want to stir up old memories. I thought it would be easier for both of us if I left it in the past.”

As we sat in silence, I tried to swallow the hurt, but doubts lingered. Was I his present—or merely a placeholder for a love he had never fully let go of?

I wanted to trust him, to believe in our bond. But the shadows of his past had seeped into the foundation of our future, and for the first time, I wondered if love alone would be enough to overcome them.

V

Stirrings

The sun rose gently over the horizon, casting its golden light over a city brimming with excitement. Today was the day—my wedding day.

Outside, the air vibrated with joyful anticipation as guests began to arrive, dressed in vibrant saris and elegant suits. The sound of laughter mingled with the rhythmic beat of the wedding drums, filling the air with a festive spirit. Flowers adorned every corner, their delicate scent weaving through the lively chatter and music.

Inside, I sat before the mirror, my heart pounding. Maggi stood beside me, adjusting the folds of my saree, her hands trembling slightly. She stepped back, her eyes shimmering with emotion. "Satya, you look beautiful." she whispered, her voice thick with tears.

Just then, my mom entered the room. She paused, taking in the sight of me in my bridal attire, her expression a mix of pride and nostalgia. She walked over, her smile tender as she brushed a stray lock of hair from my face. "My baby, you're getting married today," she murmured, her own eyes glassy.

I stood, my hands smoothing down the intricate embroidery on my saree as I took a deep breath, trying to steady my nerves. My mind swirled with a whirlwind of emotions—joy, excitement, and a shadow of lingering uncertainty.

Maggi squeezed my hand. “Satya, I know you’re nervous. But today is your day. No doubts, okay? Just let yourself be happy.”

I smiled, grateful for her strength. For now, I set aside the questions that had been haunting me and focused on the love surrounding me—the warmth of my family, the support of my friends, and the promise of a new beginning.

As I made my way to the ceremony, the world around me faded into a blur. All I could hear was the beat of my heart, a rhythm matching the wedding drums. I whispered a silent prayer, hoping that the doubts that had lingered would dissolve into the happiness of this moment.

Today, I would take a step forward, leaving my fears behind—ready to face whatever came next, one heartbeat at a time.

Downstairs, voices echoed through the hallway, punctuating the festive atmosphere with tension. Vittal’s father, Rao, stood at the center of a growing crowd, his voice sharp and unyielding.

“I expect nothing but the best for my son,” he declared, his words thick with entitlement. “The dowry we agreed upon isn’t sufficient. I want an additional 5 lakhs.”

My father’s face flushed with indignation. “We’ve already given all we can. We’ve stretched beyond our means. There’s nothing more we can give.”

Rao sneered, unfazed. “If you want to be part of our family, you’ll do as we say.”

The words hung heavy in the air, the weight of their meaning pressing on everyone in the room. Vittal appeared, his face strained as he took in the scene. "Father, please. This isn't the time for this. Today is about us, about family."

Rao barely spared him a glance, his tone dismissive. "You'll understand when you're older, son. This is how things are done. This is business."

I felt a surge of horror as I watched the argument grow heated, the joy of the day overshadowed by greed and demands. My heart raced, each word and accusation chipping away at the foundation of what I thought our marriage would be.

This was more than a momentary outburst—this was a glimpse into a truth I hadn't been ready to face. The ideals I cherished, the love I thought we were building, all felt as if they were being tested.

As I stood before Vittal, my heart pounding, we exchanged vows. His gaze held mine, warm and intense, but beneath it, my mind swirled with questions that refused to quiet. Madhu's name echoed in my thoughts, her presence a ghost between us. What promise had he made to her, and why was it haunting me now, in this sacred moment?

The priest's words became a distant hum, overshadowed by the unease growing in my chest. I forced a smile, searching Vittal's face for reassurance, for a sign that I was the one he truly wanted. But doubt lingered, cold and unsettling. I couldn't ignore the chasm between our families, the endless demands for dowry, the feeling that love was only part of this complex equation.

As Vittal reached to tie the sacred thread around my neck, symbolizing our bond, a shiver ran down my spine. This was the commitment that would bind us, and yet a small, insistent voice within me asked: was I stepping into a life of love, or was I about to become an unwitting participant in someone else's unfinished story?

I found myself making a silent promise of my own: I will honor this bond. But I will also honor myself.

And as Vittal slipped his hand into mine once more, I knew that whatever lay ahead, I would face it—not with blind devotion, but with eyes wide open.

The ceremony unfolded like a beautiful, bittersweet dream—a whirlwind of color, song, and sacred vows. Each ritual passed in a haze, my hands moving in time with tradition, yet my heart felt weighed down with doubts I couldn't dismiss.

As the sun dipped, casting a soft, golden light over the crowd, we completed our final vows. We were husband and wife. Yet, amid the joy and blessings, a shadow hung between us—a question left unspoken, an uncertainty that lingered in Vittal's distant gaze and the demanding presence of his family.

The evening continued with laughter, cheerful voices rising in celebration, and flashes of the camera capturing our smiles. Vittal's arm rested around me, his touch warm, but his smile didn't reach his eyes. As we posed for photos, I felt a pang of loneliness, a sense of standing alone, even in his embrace.

A swirl of questions circled my mind: Could our love survive the expectations placed on it? Was there room for us, for who we truly were, within these walls built on tradition and material desires?

The night grew late, and as we prepared to leave, I glanced back at the decorated mandap where we had exchanged our vows, wondering what lay ahead. Beneath the music and festivity, I sensed the stirrings of an oncoming storm.

VI

Leap of faith

The journey to Vittal's home had been filled with hopes of warmth and new beginnings. But as I stepped into the grand estate, an unfamiliar chill swept over me. The lavish decor and ornate architecture stood in sharp contrast to the tension in the air. Vittal guided me upstairs to our room, his attempts at reassurance clear in his gentle touch and soft words. Yet, beneath his calm demeanor, I sensed an unease—a hint of tension flickering in his eyes.

The room itself was beautiful, filled with fragrant flowers and intricate designs, yet I couldn't shake the feeling that I was an outsider in this house, more a guest than family. "You'll love it here, Satya," Vittal murmured as he helped me settle. I wanted to believe him, to think that our life here could be one of happiness and partnership, but the lingering shadows of our wedding day cast doubt over my thoughts.

Downstairs, the stillness shattered as Rao's voice boomed through the hallways, his words cutting through the evening calm. His words, directed at my father, echoed up the stairs, each syllable like a stone dropped into a quiet lake, sending ripples of unease through me.

“You deceived us, Murthy. The arrangements were disgraceful, and the dowry was insufficient. I expected far better,” he seethed. My father’s steady, calm response followed, though I could tell even from a distance that he was trying to keep his composure. "We gave all we could, Rao," he said with quiet dignity. "Satya’s happiness is what we value most."

Rao’s response was chilling. “Her happiness? That’s not your concern any longer. She’s part of our family now, and she’ll abide by our rules.Satya will never set foot in your house again.” The words felt like a cold slap, a reminder of the control they sought to exert. In one sentence, Rao had erased the love and freedom I had known, replacing it with possessiveness and expectations.

As the call ended, I imagined my parents exchanging a look of shared worry, their love for me mingling with fear. "We just want Satya to be happy," my mother had murmured, her voice barely a whisper, filled with all the tenderness and concern that only a parent could feel. My father nodded, his face resolute. "We’ll do everything in our power to keep her safe," he replied, making a silent promise, even as he worried about whether he’d be able to keep it.

Little did I know, their words would become a vow, one that would be tested time and time again in the months to come

Vittal’s grip around me tightened, as if by holding me closer he could shield me from the truths I sensed were lurking beneath the surface. For a long moment, he said nothing, his gaze flickering to the ceiling, lost in thought.

Finally, he sighed, a weary sound that seemed to carry the weight of his own hidden struggles. “Satya,” he began, his voice barely above a whisper, “I know my father’s demands have made this difficult for you. I wish I could change things. Believe me, I do."

"But what about Madhu?" The name felt heavy on my tongue, carrying all my fears, insecurities, and unanswered questions. "What promise did you make to her?"

He sat up, running a hand through his hair, his face shadowed in the dim light. "Madhu was... someone important to me once. We shared a past, but that's all it is—a past. Whatever I promised her, it doesn't affect you and me, Satya. You're my future."

Though his words were meant to reassure me, they left a hollow ache. "But why didn't you tell me before?" I asked, feeling raw and exposed. "Why keep these secrets?"

Vittal's sudden anger stunned me, his words slicing through the room like a blade. "You're still questioning me about Madhu?" he demanded, his voice reverberating off the walls. The warmth in his eyes had vanished, replaced by a cold, piercing glare that left me breathless. "Can't you see I'm trying to move on, to start anew with you?"

I stepped back, my heart pounding. The sharpness of his tone was a shock—a side of him I hadn't seen, one that was fierce, unyielding. "I just want the truth," I managed, my voice trembling but determined. This wasn't about accusing him. It was about understanding the person I'd promised my life to.

"The truth?" he spat, his lips twisting in a sneer. "You're my wife now, Satya. You'll learn to trust me, to obey me, without questioning every word I say."

The sting of his words left me speechless, my confidence dissolving into confusion. My chest tightened, and tears prickled at the corners of my eyes. Before I could gather the strength to respond, his expression softened, the anger dissipating as suddenly as it had come. He reached out, wrapping me in a gentle embrace, his tone shifting like a storm giving way to a deceptive calm.

"Satya, forgive me," he whispered, his lips brushing against my ear in a gesture that felt oddly both soothing and unsettling. "I didn't mean to scare you. You're my everything now."

I remained still in his arms, my heart racing for an entirely different reason. The speed of his change, from fury to tenderness, left me spinning. Just moments ago, he was boiling over with rage. Now, his hand caressed my back, tracing gentle, deliberate patterns. His breath warmed my neck as he pressed me closer, as if trying to erase the sting of his anger with an unexpected rush of affection.

"Let's put the past behind us," he murmured, each word a lull that tugged at my desire to believe him. "We'll start anew, just us. No more questions, no more doubts."

His voice was soft, almost hypnotic, weaving a spell of confusion and longing. I wanted so desperately to believe him, to let go of the unease growing inside me. But there was something in his gaze, a flicker of desperation he couldn't quite hide, as if he was grasping at a fragile thread he feared would break.

"Vittal," I whispered, barely finding my voice, "who are you, really?"

He looked at me then, a small smile playing on his lips, his eyes crinkling at the corners in that familiar, charming way. "I'm your husband, Satya. Your partner, your friend. That's all that matters."

I wanted to hold on to that smile, to let it wash away my fears. But as his words sank in, I felt an unsettling realization gnaw at the edges of my mind. His smile, warm and reassuring, felt more like a mask than a revelation. And in that moment, I knew: Vittal was hiding something deep, something darker than I'd ever imagined.

The air between us felt thick with tension, his arms wrapped around me in a way that felt both comforting and suffocating. My heart raced, torn between the love I'd always dreamed of and the reality unfolding before me. Vittal's mood swung like a pendulum, from rage to tenderness, leaving me disoriented and questioning everything.

I tried to pull back to catch my breath, but he held me closer, his grip firm. "Satya," he murmured, his tone gentler now, almost pleading, "We have the rest of our lives to get to know each other. Stop dwelling on the past. Let it go, for us."

His words echoed, each one entangled with promises of love and loyalty, yet shadowed by an unspoken warning. I wanted to believe him, to think that his anger was a passing storm, one that would fade with time. But I couldn't ignore the creeping doubt. Vittal's fierce reaction, his insistence that I obey him without question—these were glimpses into a side of him I hadn't known existed.

"Can we really leave the past behind?" I asked, my voice quivering. "What about your family's expectations? The dowry, the things they've demanded... I feel like I'm just a part of some transaction."

His face softened, though I noticed a flicker of irritation. "My family is my family, Satya, but I'm the one you married. Whatever they've said or done, it doesn't matter to me. What matters is us." He brushed a tear from my cheek, his fingers lingering as though he could erase my fears with a single touch.

Yet even as he said the words, I sensed he was holding something back. His hand lingered on my cheek, his gaze intense, and for a fleeting moment, he seemed vulnerable, like a man grappling with his own demons.

"I want to believe you," I said, voice barely a whisper. "But trust can't just be demanded. It has to be earned."

His jaw tightened, the softness evaporating. "Maybe," he replied, a shadow crossing his face. "But sometimes love means having faith, even when you don't understand everything. Can you do that for me, Satya?"

The question hung in the air, weighted with expectations. And as I looked into his eyes, searching for the truth beneath his words, I realized that this was a leap of faith I'd have to take—whether or not I was ready.

I nodded slowly, though my heart remained conflicted. As he held me close, I wondered if my promise of trust would be enough. Or if, one day, it would leave me broken.

As the night wore on, Vittal's mood shifted again, his eyes burning with a desire that made me uneasy. He pulled me closer, his hands tracing the contours of my body, his lips whispering sweet nothings in my ear.

At first, I tried to reciprocate, to match his passion with my own. But his touch felt suffocating, his kisses overwhelming. I pushed against his chest, trying to create some space.

"Vittal, please...I need some time," I whispered, my voice trembling.

But he didn't listen. His hands roamed my body, his fingers probing, insisting. I felt a wave of panic rise up, my heart racing with fear.

"Vittal, stop...please," I begged, trying to squirm free.

But he was relentless, his mouth crushing mine, his body pinning me down. Tears streamed down my face as I realized he wasn't going to stop.

"Why are you doing this?" I sobbed, my voice muffled against his chest.

He didn't respond, his actions speaking louder than words. I felt trapped, helpless, as he continued to force his desires upon me.

My mind raced back to our conversation, his words echoing in my mind: "Sometimes love means having faith, even when you don't understand everything." But this wasn't love; this was possession.

I felt my body numb, my spirit crushed. Vittal's passion was a facade, a mask hiding a darker truth. I realized I was married to a stranger, a man who didn't care about my consent or my feelings.

The tears I shed were not just for the physical pain but for the shattering of my dreams, for the loss of the love I thought we shared. As the darkness closed in, I knew I had to find a way to escape, to reclaim my life from this suffocating grip.

But for now, I lay trapped, my body trembling beneath his, my heart crying out for help that seemed impossible to find.In that moment, something inside me changed. The love I'd held for him, fragile as it was, crumbled. My heart screamed, a silent plea swallowed by the oppressive silence of the room. I fought back tears, knowing that to show them would only weaken me further in his eyes.

As dawn began to paint the sky outside, I lay beside him, hollow and numb. My body felt like a vessel emptied of spirit, a puppet held by strings I hadn't agreed to. I stared at the ceiling, thoughts swirling in my mind like a storm, the remnants of my dreams swept away.

VII

Lady of the house

The night had left me shattered, my soul bruised and battered. Sleep, once a refuge, now eluded me as I lay beside Vittal, my thoughts racing like storm clouds, restless and fierce. My body ached from the unspoken tension between us, but my mind was far worse—torn between the suffocating weight of my reality and the distant flickers of an old dream: escape, freedom, the life I thought I might have had.

But with dawn came the harsh clarity of my situation. The sun crept through the heavy curtains, casting long, indifferent shadows across the room. It was as if the light itself mocked me—reminding me that another day had begun, another day I was trapped.

Every day felt like a repetition of the last, the monotony erasing any sense of time.Each morning, Vittal would leave for work with a perfunctory kiss on my forehead, a routine gesture devoid of warmth or meaning. And then, I was left alone, abandoned to the sprawling emptiness of the estate. The house, though magnificent in its size, seemed more like a tomb. The silence of it suffocated me. My mother-in-law, Rao's wife, had become my shadow. She had appointed herself the keeper of my fate, ensuring that I knew my place in the hierarchy of this house.

"Satya, you're the lady of the house now," she would say, her tone thin and laced with an air of false benevolence. "It's your responsibility to manage everything here. You understand, don't you?"

Her words stung. There was no warmth, no tenderness in them—only a reminder that I was now nothing more than a servant, my existence defined by the demands of a family I no longer recognized.

The tasks were endless. Cooking, cleaning, tending to the house as though it were a living thing that needed constant care. Not a single maid or servant in sight to help lighten the load. It was as if I had been set up to fail, expected to be everywhere, do everything, and yet never be enough.

By evening, Vittal would return—his presence as predictable as the setting sun. Dinner would be served, consumed without conversation, and then he would turn his attention to me. His attempts at intimacy felt like a mechanical ritual, as though he was trying to reclaim a part of me that had never truly existed for him. I was no longer his wife in the way I once had been, but something else—an object, a fixture in the house.

I went through the motions, like an actress on a stage, performing a part I didn't know how to leave. There was no passion, no joy, just the numbness of routine, of a life I had never chosen. My heart had retreated deep inside me, a shell protecting what was left of my spirit. I had become a ghost in my own life, watching it unfold without ever truly living it.

In the rare moments when I was alone, the quiet would settle over me like a weight. Tears would come, silent and unbidden, as if my soul could no longer hold the unbearable truth of what I had become. I cried for the girl I used to be, the girl who had dreams, who had hopes. I cried for the freedom that had slipped through my fingers like sand. I cried for my parents, for the home I had left behind, for the life I had been forced to abandon.

It was during one of these moments, standing in the kitchen, the smell of simmering spices thick in the air, that I caught a glimpse of myself in the window's reflection. The face staring back at me was a stranger's. Hollow-eyed, gaunt, and pale. Her skin had lost its warmth, her eyes devoid of the spark that had once defined her. She was someone I barely recognized. Someone I didn't want to be.

"How did I end up here?" I whispered to the glass, my voice barely audible, as if afraid the question might shatter what was left of me.

The reflection didn't answer, of course. It only stared back in its silent, indifferent way. The stillness was deafening, suffocating. I didn't need an answer. I already knew it. I had allowed myself to be swallowed whole by a life I hadn't chosen, by promises that had turned into lies.

I had to find a way out. A way to break free. The chains that bound me to this house, to this life, were invisible, but no less real. They tightened with every passing day, constricting my breath, dimming my soul. I couldn't stay here, trapped in a gilded cage of expectations.

But for now, there was no escape. Only this suffocating existence, this endless night that seemed to stretch on forever.

As darkness fell again, Vittal's arms found me, pulling me close in a gesture that felt more like an obligation than affection. His breath, hot and insistent, whispered promises he did not mean. His touch, once a source of comfort, now felt like a cruel reminder of the life I had lost, the life that seemed so far beyond my reach.

I lay still, my body unmoving, my heart screaming silently in the cage of my chest. I could feel the weight of it, the heaviness of the silence between us, and the deeper silence within me. My soul searched the darkness for any glimmer of hope, any flicker of a life that was still mine to claim.

But there was nothing. Only the endless night, and the cruel rhythm of a life that refused to let me go.

On that fateful evening, Vittal lurched into the house, the heavy scent of alcohol hanging around him. His movements were jerky, uncoordinated, as if his body had forgotten how to function properly. His eyes were glassy and distant, vacant in a way that sent a chill down my spine. He took a few unsteady steps, his hands brushing the walls for support, before his gaze landed on me.

I stood frozen, watching in horror as he lurched toward me. His parents, as usual, were nowhere to be found—either ignorant of or indifferent to the chaos unfolding in their own home. Not a single word of concern crossed their lips. No reprimand for their son, no inquiry into his state. It was as if they had grown numb to the sight of his drunken stupors, as though they had accepted his behavior as part of the family's fabric, woven into the very walls of this house.

"Satya," he slurred, his voice low and thick with contempt. "You think you're so perfect, don't you?" The words dripped from his mouth like poison. He swayed unsteadily, his hand reaching out toward me in a half-hearted grab. "You think you can just sit there and judge me?"

I recoiled, fear tightening its grip around my chest. My heart pounded in my throat. “Vittal, please...stop. You’re drunk. Go to bed.”

But he didn’t listen. His face contorted with something darker than mere inebriation—something sharp, something cruel. He took another step closer, his body leaning into mine. "You’re my wife," he growled, and you’ll do what I say. You’ll obey me, no matter what."

My breath hitched in my chest as panic rose. I could feel the weight of his words, their coldness suffocating. He lunged at me, his hands clawing, desperate, and I stumbled backward, my back hitting the edge of the bed.

I fought, struggling against his grip as he forced me onto the mattress. His body pressed down on me, heavy and oppressive, like a thousand tons of stone. My breath came in shallow gasps, my mind screaming for escape, but there was nowhere to go.

Tears blurred my vision as I realized how powerless I truly was. He was too strong, too much. I couldn’t move. I couldn’t scream. I was trapped beneath him, my world narrowing to the suffocating weight of his body, the stench of alcohol, the heat of his breath.

In a burst of desperation, I summoned every ounce of strength I had left. My arms shot upward, my legs pushing against his chest, trying to break free. With a grunt of effort, I shoved him with all the power in my body.

For a moment, there was silence—his stunned expression, his mouth slightly open, as if he couldn’t believe I’d dared to resist him. Then, like a switch had been flipped, his face twisted into a mask of fury.

“You dare to defy me?” he roared, his voice a thunderclap that reverberated in my chest.

Before I could react, his hand whipped through the air, striking my cheek with a sharp crack that sent a shockwave through my body. The pain exploded across my face, and everything around me seemed to blur. My ears rang. My vision darkened.

"You'll pay for that," he growled, his voice full of venom, and his eyes—those glassy, hateful eyes—burned into mine with an intensity that made my blood run cold.

He was on me again in a heartbeat, his hands grabbing my arms and pinning them above my head. He forced me down, his weight crushing my chest, each breath a struggle. My cries, my pleas—everything I said was drowned in the suffocating night. My body thrashed, but his hold on me was unyielding.

The room spun as I struggled against him, but the weight of his anger, his physicality, was too much. His hands, now rough and merciless, dug into my skin, leaving marks where they shouldn't be. His mouth was everywhere—on my neck, my shoulders, his breath hot and foul.

The night stretched on, and with it, the violence and terror. I lost track of time—how long had it been? Minutes? Hours? It didn't matter. The pain blurred into one continuous, never-ending agony. My body, my mind, all faded into the darkness. I was no longer aware of where I ended and the night began.

When it was finally over, I lay there, broken and spent, my body trembling uncontrollably. My skin felt raw, bruised, every inch of me ached as though I'd been torn apart. Vittal, on the other hand, had passed out beside me, his snores heavy and deep, oblivious to the destruction he had left behind.

The contrast was unbearable. His deep, untroubled sleep was a cruel mockery of the hell I had just endured. I wanted to scream. I wanted to rage. But I was too exhausted, too broken to do anything but lie there in the dark, unable to move, unable to escape.

The weight of it all pressed down on me—so heavy, so suffocating. I was lost, swallowed by the crushing reality of my life. I had no escape. No way out. No one to turn to.

In that moment, I realized I wasn't just trapped by my circumstances, by this house, by Vittal's cruelty. I had been trapped long before, by my own hopes and dreams, by the false promises I had believed. There was no key to unlock my freedom.

I had lost myself—piece by piece, moment by moment.

And now, I was just a ghost, lingering in the remains of a life I could never have.

VIII
Shattered

Days blended together in a haze of pain and fear. I went through the motions, pretending to be the dutiful wife, hiding the truth behind a mask of normalcy. But the memory of that fateful night lingered, a constant reminder of my vulnerability.

I longed to share my secret with someone, anyone, who could understand my pain. My parents, perhaps, or a friend. But the thought of their sorrow, their helplessness, kept me silent. I couldn't bear the weight of their worry, the guilt of knowing they couldn't save me.

So I suffered alone, trapped in this prison of expectations.

Then, one day, my parents arrived unexpectedly, their faces etched with concern. They brought gifts, including a substantial sum of money, hoping to appease Rao and maintain the fragile peace.

But as they entered our grand estate, their expressions changed. They saw me, pale and gaunt, my eyes sunken, my spirit crushed. The facade of normalcy crumbled, revealing the truth beneath.

"Satya...." my mother whispered, her voice trembling. "What's happening? You look...different."

I forced a smile, desperate to shield them from the reality. "I'm fine, ma. Just tired. Taking care of the house is a lot of work."

But they saw through my lies. Their eyes, filled with a mix of sadness and helplessness, met mine. They knew. They understood.

My father's jaw clenched, his fists tightening. "We should take you home," he said, his voice low and urgent.

I shook my head, fear gripping my heart. "No, Appa. Please. It's not safe. Vittal...he won't let me go."

My mother's hands wrapped around mine, warm and comforting. "We'll figure something out, Satya. We won't leave you here like this."

But I knew better. Rao's influence, Vittal's control – it was a web too intricate to untangle. My parents' presence only made things worse, risking Vittal's wrath.

"Please, Ma, Appa," I begged, tears streaming down my face. "Don't make things worse. Just go. I'll be fine."

Their faces twisted in anguish, but they knew I was right. They couldn't save me, not now. Not here.

As they prepared to leave, my father pressed the money into Rao's hands, a futile attempt to placate him. "For Satya's well-being," he said, his voice strained.

Rao's smile, cold and calculating, sent shivers down my spine. "Thank you, Murthy. Your generosity is appreciated."

My parents departed, leaving me with a sense of desperation. I knew I had to find a way out, before it was too late. But for now, I remained trapped, a pawn in a game I didn't know how to play.

As the door closed behind them, Vittal emerged from the shadows, his eyes narrowing. "What did they want?" he asked, his tone laced with suspicion.

I shrugged, feigning indifference. "Just a visit. They brought some money for your father."

His gaze lingered on me, searching for any sign of betrayal. "Good," he said finally. "We'll need it."

The darkness closed in around me once more, suffocating me with its crushing weight. I knew I had to escape, but the path ahead seemed impossible to navigate.

In the days that followed, my parents' visit became a haunting memory, a flicker of warmth in the cold reality I now called life. Their departure left me feeling both hopelessly trapped and deeply resolute. I had no illusions left—this was no marriage but a masquerade, and I was merely a player in a cruel game orchestrated by Vittal and his family.

Vittal grew colder, his suspicion seeping into every interaction. He watched me closely, as if expecting me to rebel, to dare resist the invisible chains he'd bound me with. And yet, I kept up the charade, pretending to be the obedient wife, all while nurturing a growing ember of defiance deep within me.

In the quiet moments, I found myself drawn to the small mirror in our room, searching my own eyes for strength. Where had that spark gone? The girl who dreamed, who laughed easily, who believed in love? I knew that if I could summon her again, I might have a chance. I might find a way out.

࿇

One evening, after Vittal had left for yet another one of his meetings, his parents were sleeping. I slipped out of the house for peace. My hands trembled as I locked the door behind me, every creak of the latch sounding like thunder in the oppressive silence of the night. The narrow streets were cloaked in shadows, but I walked them with a heart pounding so fiercely it felt as though it might burst from my chest. Each step was a fragile act of rebellion, a daring gamble against the suffocating confines of my existence.

The streets stretched endlessly, but I moved with purpose, driven by an unseen force. My destination was a temple near my house —a sanctuary where the world seemed to pause, where the noise of my chaotic life faded into the background. The temple, nestled beneath a canopy of ancient banyan trees, exuded an aura of peace. Its golden glow, cast by countless flickering deepam, wrapped around me like a protective embrace.

I sat cross-legged on the cool stone floor, surrounded by the faint aroma of incense and the gentle hum of devotees' prayers. The stillness seeped into me, quieting the storm raging within. As I closed my eyes, a flood of memories washed over me—the laughter I had lost, the dreams I had buried, and the person I once was but could no longer recognize.

It was here, in this sacred space, that a fierce determination began to take root. I didn't know how, or when, or even if I could succeed, but I knew with every fiber of my being that I had to escape. The life I was living wasn't mine; it was a shadow, a prison. I had to reclaim my voice, my freedom, and the essence of who I was before it was completely consumed by the darkness surrounding me.

The path ahead was fraught with danger. I would face obstacles that seemed insurmountable and betrayals that would cut deeper than any wound. Yet, as fear whispered its insidious warnings, a stronger voice—the voice of my soul—spoke louder. It reminded me that I had endured so much already. And if I could survive this long, I could also fight.

Returning to the house that night, I wore a mask of calm, though every fiber of my being was alight with the quiet fire of rebellion. I moved carefully, methodically, as though stepping on glass, wary of any slip that might give away the battle raging within me.

༺

One morning, as I was cleaning the living room, I noticed Vittal's phone lying on the couch. He had forgotten it in his haste to leave for work. My heart skipped a beat as I picked it up, feeling a sudden sense of freedom.

I hadn't spoken to my parents since their visit, and the longing to hear their voices had become unbearable. I decided to use Vittal's phone to call them, hoping to find some solace in our conversation.

As I scrolled through his contacts, my eyes landed on a name that made my heart stutter: Madhu.

Curiosity got the better of me, and I opened the messaging app. The notification icon indicated unread messages. My hands trembled as I clicked on the conversation.

The words on the screen blurred together, but one phrase stood out: "Can't wait to see you tonight, my love." My vision began to tunnel, focusing on the message. Vittal's response: "I'll be waiting. Missing you."

I scrolled further, my stomach churning with each passing message. The intimacy was palpable, the affection clear. They were more than just friends.

And then, I saw them. Videos. Intimate videos of Vittal and Madhu together. My mind reeled, unable to process the betrayal.

I felt like I'd been punched in the gut, my breath knocked out of me. Tears streamed down my face as I stumbled backward, collapsing onto the couch.

The pain was overwhelming, a tidal wave crashing over me. I sobbed uncontrollably, my body shaking with each ragged breath.

How could he? How could he do this to me? To our marriage?

All this time, I thought I was just trapped in a loveless marriage, burdened by household chores and loneliness. But this...this was a different kind of prison.

I was a fool, blinded by my own desperation to make this marriage work. Vittal's infidelity cut deeper than any knife, leaving me bleeding and exposed.

As the tears slowly subsided, leaving behind a dull ache, I realized I had two options: succumb to the pain or find a way to escape.

I looked around the room, the opulent furniture and decorations mocking me. This wasn't my home. This was my cage.

With newfound determination, I wiped away my tears. I would not be held captive by Vittal's deceit. I would find a way out, no matter the cost.

The discovery felt like a wound tearing open, raw and uncontainable. I sat there, Vittal's phone clutched in my hand, each message cutting deeper than the last. The betrayal—those moments of intimacy, the promises he shared with Madhu—tore apart any remnants of hope I'd held for our marriage. This wasn't just infidelity. This was a carefully constructed lie, spun around me while I fought to be the dutiful wife in a marriage he never respected.

As I sat on the couch, memories came flooding back—the small things I'd overlooked, the evasive answers, his temper flaring whenever I asked about Madhu. Now, everything made sense. His hollow reassurances, his family's coldness, the oppressive atmosphere of this household—they were all threads of the same dark truth. My life here had been a mirage.

In a moment of despair, I wanted to break down, to let the pain overtake me. But a voice inside reminded me that I'd shed enough tears, endured enough agony in silence. Vittal and his family had underestimated me, treated me as something fragile and disposable. But I was stronger than they realized.

A fierce determination ignited within me. This marriage was my cage, but I would find a way out. My parents' faces came to mind—their silent sorrow, the love they'd shown me even as they felt powerless to protect me. I would not return to them as a broken shell of myself. I would find my way out of this, not just for me, but for them, too.

With newfound resolve, I scrolled through the messages once more, reading every detail of Vittal's exchanges with Madhu, cataloging them in my memory. If I was to escape, I'd need leverage, something to guard against the wrath Vittal and his family might unleash if I tried to leave.

I tucked the phone back where I'd found it, my heart pounding with a strange mix of fear and empowerment. This wouldn't be easy, and I knew I would face challenges beyond anything I'd ever known. But I wasn't going to be trapped in this deception any longer.

In the coming days, I would have to be meticulous, discreet. Every glance, every movement, every conversation would be part of my strategy. My trust in Vittal had shattered, but in its place grew a steely determination to reclaim my life.

As I stood and steadied myself, I looked around the room—this ornate, hollow cage Vittal called home.

IX

Beneath the Surface

That evening, Vittal returned home, his face drawn and weary from a long day at work. There was a heaviness in his step, as if the world outside had taken a toll on him, but I could see it— the familiar indifference, the way he shut himself off from anything that might require emotional investment. It was a mask I had come to know all too well. As he stepped inside, the door thudded shut behind him, but I was already standing in the kitchen, my heart hammering in my chest. The secrets I'd uncovered on his phone still burned in my mind, the images and messages seared into my thoughts like a brand. And the rage... the rage simmered under my skin, threatening to erupt.

"Vittal," I called out, my voice steady despite the chaos inside. "We need to talk."

He glanced up, his eyes narrowing as he saw me standing there. The lines of his face were drawn with exhaustion, but I could tell his mind was already retreating into a defensive shell. The walls were going up, and I wasn't sure if I'd be able to break through them.

"What's the matter?" His voice was thick with a mix of annoyance and weariness. He wasn't surprised by my request, but he was clearly irritated. That was what I had become to him: an inconvenient problem to avoid.

I inhaled deeply, gathering every ounce of strength I had left. This was it. There could be no turning back now. "Madhu. Who is she?"

The words hung in the air, sharp and heavy, and for a brief moment, I saw his expression falter. There was something—something he couldn't quite hide—that flickered in his eyes. But then, like a well-practiced actor, he quickly regained his composure, putting up the mask that had always protected him.

"Just a friend," he said, his tone dismissive, too rehearsed to be believable. He tried to brush me off, but I could already feel the tension tightening between us.

I clenched my fists, my nails digging into my palms as the anger threatened to boil over. "Don't lie to me, Vittal," I spat, unable to hold back the fury anymore. "I saw the messages. The videos. I know everything."

His jaw tightened, the muscles in his face working as if trying to suppress the sudden shift in his expression. But his eyes—those cold, calculating eyes—gave him away. He was trying to contain something. Panic? Fear? Maybe even guilt. But he didn't dare show it. Instead, he turned on me, his voice now hard, like a slap.

"You were snooping through my phone?" he snarled, his anger rising as he took a step closer, his eyes dark with rage.

I didn't flinch. "I wasn't snooping," I said, my voice rising with a fury that seemed to have a life of its own. "I was looking for something—anything—to hold on to. But instead, I found your lies. Your betrayal. How long, Vittal? How long has this been going on?"

The air between us crackled with electricity, thick and charged. The words hung in the space, reverberating through the walls of our home, and for a brief moment, I could almost feel the weight of everything we'd built crashing down around us.

He took another step forward, his nostrils flaring, eyes flashing with an anger that I could feel in my gut. "That's none of your business," he hissed, his tone laced with venom.

I stood my ground, my heart pounding with the force of a thousand storms. "It is my business," I shot back, my voice gaining strength with every word. "I'm your wife, or have you forgotten? You don't get to treat me like this."

His face contorted, his fists tightening at his sides. He was losing control, and I could see it. The man who had always felt entitled, who had always used his strength to dominate, was now being forced to face something that couldn't be solved with arrogance and dismissal. He opened his mouth to speak, but the words came out in a low, dangerous growl.

"You'll do well to remember your place," he warned, his voice dripping with menace.

The fear I'd once felt in his presence—the fear that had once paralyzed me—began to dissolve. It was replaced by something sharper, something colder. I lifted my chin, meeting his gaze with unwavering resolve. "My place?" I repeated, the words cold as ice. "My place is not as your puppet. Not as your prisoner."

The room seemed to freeze for a moment, both of us locked in a silent battle, his anger and my defiance. For the first time, I saw the cracks in his armor, the uncertainty behind the mask. And for the first time, I felt something shift inside me—something that had been buried deep, something I didn't even know I had.

I wasn't the woman who would silently endure anymore.

I wasn't the wife who would stay silent in the face of betrayal.

He wasn't the man who could control me.

I could feel the weight of his gaze on me, the heat of his anger burning into me, but I didn't care anymore. The truth had come to light, and no amount of his threats, no amount of his rage, could erase what had already been uncovered.

"You think you can break me?" I said, my voice low, but with a defiance that shook the air around us. "You think you can control me with your lies?"

Vittal opened his mouth to respond, but no words came. He stood there, frozen, as if he hadn't expected me to fight back. But there was no going back now. My life, my future—it was mine again. And no matter what happened next, I wouldn't let him steal that from me.

I turned away from him, the silence between us now louder than any argument could be. My body trembled with the adrenaline, but I felt a strange sense of clarity. I had fought for my dignity, my truth. And for the first time, I didn't feel like I was the one who had lost.

Vittal's face contorted with fury, his hands balling into fists at his sides. The mask he'd so carefully worn cracked, revealing a side of him I hadn't seen so plainly before: ruthless, unyielding, and utterly without remorse.

He took a step closer, his gaze hard and unrelenting. "You don't get to make demands here, Satya," he said, his voice low but charged. "You are my wife. And as far as I'm concerned, that means you do as I say. You owe me respect, not accusations."

A bitter laugh escaped me, breaking through my fear. "Respect? You talk about respect, but you don't have any for me, or for this marriage. You've treated me like a commodity, like an accessory to impress your you and your family. Well, I won't play that part anymore."

For a moment, something flickered in his eyes, a sliver of doubt perhaps. But it vanished as quickly as it had come. "What are you going to do, Satya?" he sneered, his tone laced with contempt. "Run home to your parents? Leave with nothing but your pride? Trust me, they can't protect you from me."

I took a deep breath, steadying myself. "Maybe you think I'm trapped, Vittal. Maybe you think your money and your family's influence make you untouchable. But you're wrong. I may have come here as your wife, but I won't stay here as your prisoner."

He laughed, a cold, mocking sound. "Is that so? Where will you go, Satya? Without me, you're nothing. Just another discarded woman with nowhere to turn."

I met his gaze, my voice calm but resolute. "I'd rather be that than stay here with a man who sees me as nothing more than an object. If you think I'll tolerate your lies and betrayals, you're mistaken."

Vittal's sneer faded, replaced by a calculating look. "Fine, Satya," he said, his tone dripping with disdain. "Play the martyr. But don't expect me to save you when you come crawling back, begging for a place here."

I stood firm, feeling an unexpected sense of clarity. "I won't beg, Vittal. And I won't crawl. I'm leaving, with or without your blessing."

As he stormed out of the kitchen, slamming the door behind him, a strange calm settled over me. For the first time, I felt the weight of my own strength—a strength I'd never acknowledged until now. I didn't know where this journey would take me or what battles lay ahead. But one thing was certain: I would face them on my terms, free from the shadows of his lies.

As I slammed the door behind Vittal, the sharp thud echoed through the empty hallway, reverberating in my chest. For the briefest of moments, I thought I might feel relief—freedom—a sense of victory, as though I had finally stood up for myself. The tension that had gripped me for so long seemed to dissolve, replaced by an unfamiliar sense of power. But it was fleeting.

A wave of dizziness hit me like a punch to the gut, the room spinning violently. My vision blurred, everything around me tilting as if I were falling into some bottomless abyss. My stomach churned violently, and my legs, weak and unsteady, refused to hold me up. I reached for the wall, but it felt like the floor itself was slipping away. My breath quickened, my chest tight as I tried to steady myself. The world felt like it was closing in on me, pressing in from all sides.

And then, everything went black.

X

The future

When I woke, the room was dimly lit, the silence heavy and suffocating. My head throbbed like a drumbeat, every pulse sending a shock of pain through my skull. For a moment, I didn't know where I was—just a haze of white sheets and soft linen. My vision slowly cleared, and I saw her—Vittal's mother, sitting beside me on the bed, her face contorted in concern, as if she were a stranger who had just wandered into my life.

"Satya, how are you feeling?" Her voice was soft, too soft. There was an edge of something else in it, but I couldn't quite place it. Concern? Or something darker?

I struggled to sit up, the dizziness still clouding my mind. My head swam as I reached for the edge of the bed, my hands trembling. "I... I don't know," I muttered, my voice weak and uncertain. "I just felt dizzy..." The words barely escaped my dry lips, and the nausea twisted in my stomach again.

She helped me sit up, her touch firm but too warm—too maternal, too suffocating. She placed a glass of water in my hands, but I barely had the strength to lift it. "You should rest," she said, her tone so matter-of-fact, so dismissive of the gravity of what had just happened. "You've been under a lot of stress lately."

Stress. Was that all this was? Stress?

I sipped the water slowly, but the taste in my mouth was bitter, and something gnawed at the edges of my thoughts. The dizziness wasn't just from stress—it felt different, more acute. My stomach twisted again, and then, in that moment of excruciating clarity, it hit me. A gut-wrenching, bone-deep realization that shattered me in an instant.

I was pregnant.

The thought spun my world on its axis. It was so sudden, so undeniable. The nausea. The dizziness. The ache in my body. The feeling of something inside me that couldn't be ignored any longer. I couldn't even breathe for a moment. The realization hit like a ton of bricks, and the weight of it crushed every ounce of defiance I had left.

A child. My child.

The sharp, unyielding truth of it cut through my mind like a blade.

Fear, uncertainty, and something else—something flickering like a fragile ember—rose in me. Hope? It felt so fleeting, so tentative against the overwhelming fear. But it was there, just a hint, just a whisper.

What now?

The question echoed through my head. What now? What was I supposed to do with this new truth? I could still feel the anger burning within me, the need to escape, to break free. But now... there was another life to consider. My child.

Would Vittal use our child as leverage against me? The thought was suffocating. He had shown me his worst—his rage, his cruelty. Could I trust him with a child?

And then, like a slow, suffocating fog, the harsh reality seeped in. Would I be forced to stay with him, for the sake of the baby?

Before I could process any of it, the door creaked open, and in he came—Vittal's father, like a shadow that always loomed over me. His expressions were neutral, but their eyes gleamed with something darker, something that chilled me to my core. There was no warmth, no concern. Only calculation.

"Satya, we're glad you're feeling better," Vittal's father said in that same neutral tone, his words measured, precise, like he was speaking to an employee and not his daughter-in-law. "We've been thinking..." He paused, his eyes flickering to his wife, then back to me, the weight of their unspoken intentions heavy in the air. "...with a child on the way, perhaps it's time for you and Vittal to put your differences aside."

I felt a cold shiver crawl down my spine, the words freezing me in place. They didn't know. They couldn't know. They had no idea about the infidelity, the rage that simmered beneath the surface of their perfect family. They only saw the ideal—the legacy they wanted to protect, the bloodline they wanted to continue.

A child. A son. Their grandson.

"A child is a blessing," Vittal's mother added, her voice too sweet, too eager, as if her happiness was somehow tied to the very idea of this baby. "And we're expecting a boy, of course. A son to carry on the family's legacy."

Her words wrapped around me like chains, tightening with every syllable. A son. A tool, a pawn in their game. A future that was already mapped out for him, regardless of the woman carrying him.

They didn't care about me. They didn't care about the abuse, the betrayal, the hollowness of my marriage. All they cared about was their family's reputation. Their legacy. They saw my pregnancy as a win—a victory for the family, for their name, their power.

But in that moment, I realized something far more terrifying: I was trapped.

Trapped by Vittal's rage. Trapped by his family's cold expectations. Trapped by my own vulnerability—my own helplessness.

The thought of leaving him now, of walking away with a child growing inside me, seemed impossible. What would they do to me? What would they do to my child?

My courage—the resolve I had built up—began to crumble. I wanted to leave. I wanted to fight. But now, the stakes had changed. I wasn't just fighting for myself anymore.

I have to stay. For the baby's sake.

The weight of that realization crushed me, stealing away the breath in my lungs, the fire in my veins. I had fought so hard to stand up for myself, but now I was bound—not by Vittal, not by his lies, but by something far more insidious: the quiet, suffocating love I already felt for a child I hadn't even seen yet.

My heart broke all over again as I realized the trap I was in.

I was caught.

As the realization of my pregnancy set in, a thousand emotions flooded my heart—each battling for dominance. I felt a strange and fragile hope flicker within me, an instinct to protect the tiny life growing inside. But just as quickly, the darkness of my reality washed over it, snuffing it out like a candle flame in the wind. This child, innocent and untouched by the world, would soon become another pawn in Vittal's game—a tool for control, a means to bind me further.

Vittal's mother continued to sit by my side, her gaze soft yet calculating, her hand resting on mine. "Beti," she said gently, "This child will bring you and Vittal closer. And with the family growing, it's important for you both to strengthen your bond. Sacrifices are part of marriage, you know that."

Her words echoed painfully in my mind, each one pressing down on me, making it clear that to her, I was merely a vessel for her family's legacy. I swallowed hard, struggling to mask the despair welling up inside me. How could I explain to her that Vittal's presence filled me with dread, that my so-called sacrifices had left me shattered and voiceless?

Vittal's father, standing with arms crossed, looked down at me with a steely pride. "A son will be the perfect heir to our name, Satya. And this," he said with a thin smile, "might just be the answer to all the issues between you and Vittal."

I nodded, mechanically, barely hearing them. My hand instinctively moved to my stomach, my fingers trembling. Would I truly bring my child into a world where his father was a stranger? Where love was a hollow word spoken only to maintain appearances?

As they continued discussing "The future," I found myself slipping further into despair. I tried to imagine what my life would be—raising a child in this house, under their watchful, unforgiving eyes. Vittal would likely only care about our child as a possession, an extension of his power and control. I felt the walls of the room close in, each gilded decoration mocking me, each family portrait a reminder of their ruthless expectations.

A surge of determination flared in my chest, defying the fear that threatened to consume me. I looked up, meeting Vittal's mother's gaze. "I appreciate your concern, Amma," I said, my voice steady despite the tremor I felt inside. "But I need time to process this...to understand what it means for me and my child."

Her smile faltered slightly, sensing a trace of resistance. "Of course, beti," she replied, her tone still sweet. But there was a glint in her eye—a hint that she had no intention of letting me make my own decisions. "But don't forget, a child needs both parents. And our family has certain...standards. Vittal's happiness is important to us, just as much as yours."

I nodded again, feeling the weight of their expectations settling on me like chains. But as they left the room, I took a shaky breath, a quiet promise forming in my heart. My child would not grow up in a household ruled by fear and deceit. I would find a way, even if it meant facing Vittal's fury, his family's disapproval, and the uncertainty that lay ahead.

As I lay back on the bed, my hands protectively cradling my stomach, I whispered to the little life inside me. "I'll protect you," I murmured, my voice barely audible. "No matter what it takes, I'll find a way to keep you safe."

At that moment, I knew I would need to be stronger than I had ever been before. My courage would have to be unbreakable, my love fierce enough to shatter the prison that held me. And while I didn't yet know how, I knew that somehow, I would find a way out. Not just for myself—but for my child.

XI

The past

Vittal's eyes narrowed as he sat in his study, sipping his whiskey. Satya's outburst still echoed in his mind, fueling his anger. How dare she question his authority? How dare she shout at him? The memory of her defiant tone made his grip on the glass tighten.

He couldn't care less about her pregnancy. It was just a means to an end, a way to solidify his control over her. And now, more than ever, he needed to break her spirit.

"Find out everything about her past," he instructed his loyal aide, Nagu, who stood by the door. "I want to know every secret, every weakness. Leave no stone unturned."

Nagu nodded and disappeared into the night.

Days passed, and Vittal waited impatiently for the report. When it finally arrived, he devoured the contents, his eyes scanning the pages with a mixture of curiosity and malice.

Satya's past unfolded before him like a tantalizing puzzle. Her love story before their marriage, the one she had kept hidden, now lay bare.

Karthik.

The name seared itself into Vittal's mind. Karthik, the man Satya had loved, the man she had left behind. Vittal's eyes burned with resentment as he read about their whirlwind romance, their laughter, and their tears.

He couldn't believe she had kept this from him. The audacity.

Vittal's anger simmered, boiling over as he imagined Satya with another man. He pictured Karthik's face, his smile, his touch. The thought of Satya's hands in another man's made his skin crawl.

This was war.He would use this information to destroy her, to shatter the last remnants of her defiance. Satya would regret ever crossing him.

The darkness in Vittal's heart grew, fed by his own insecurities and Satya's secrets. He would crush her and crush the very memory of their love story.

The game had begun.

ꟈ

I lay on the bed, cradling my growing belly. A quiet determination surged within me, a silent promise to protect my child and myself, no matter what. But little did I know, Vittal's revenge was just around the corner, poised to destroy the fragile hope I had begun to rebuild.

As I looked at him over those few tense days, I sensed something different. There was a new edge to his anger, a brooding intensity that unsettled me. He became unpredictable, his moods shifting from cold indifference to seething hostility. He avoided me, leaving early in the mornings and returning late at night, his eyes dark and unreadable.

Then one evening, he came home unusually early. He stood at the bedroom door, his gaze piercing as he said, "We need to talk." The undertone in his voice sent a shiver down my spine.

I took a deep breath, willing myself to appear calm. "What is it?"

He took a step closer, holding an envelope in his hand. With a cruel smile, he tossed it onto the bed in front of me. "Go on, open it."

With trembling hands, I picked up the envelope, my heart racing. I pulled out the content—photographs and love letters. I froze as I saw the familiar face staring back at me: Karthik. Memories I had tried to bury resurfaced, a bittersweet ache of a time when love had felt pure and simple.

"Karthik," he sneered, his voice dripping with disdain. "The love of your life, wasn't he? Or did you think I wouldn't find out?"

My throat went dry as I looked up, seeing the triumphant gleam in his eyes. "That's...that's in the past," I managed, my voice barely a whisper. "It has nothing to do with us, with our life now."

"Nothing to do with us?" His voice hardened as he leaned closer, his face inches from mine. "You're my wife. Your past belongs to me now. And you"—he paused, his eyes narrowing—"you're going to suffer for ever thinking you could keep secrets from me."

I gripped the sheets, my pulse roaring in my ears. I felt trapped, caged, as his malice hung in the air between us. "Vittal, please," I pleaded, searching his face for any trace of compassion. "This isn't right. Whatever I felt for Karthik was over long before we even met."

But my words only seemed to deepen his resentment. "That doesn't matter now," he replied coldly. "You will forget him. I'll make sure of it."

As he straightened and left the room, I felt a tear slip down my cheek. Shadows from my past had returned, resurrected by a man determined to control every part of me. Vittal had always treated me as an object, something he could own. Now, he would try to strip me of my last vestiges of identity, erasing the memories that had once brought me joy.

My hand drifted to my belly, seeking strength in the tiny life growing within me. "I won't let him break me," I whispered fiercely. "I'll find a way to keep you safe. No matter what he does, I'll protect you."

ജ

As the night deepened, I realized I was about to face my greatest battle yet. This wasn't just about my survival anymore—it was about creating a future, a world where my child could live freely, untouched by the cruelty that gripped Vittal's heart. And with that resolve, I knew I would have to find a way out. The stakes had risen, and my determination hardened. I would reclaim my life, for myself and for my child.

Vittal stormed out of the room, leaving me reeling from the revelation. But his departure was short-lived. He returned later, his eyes blazing with a drunken fury, a whiskey bottle clutched in his hand.

The smell of liquor filled the air as he towered over me, his voice slurring with rage. "You think you can keep secrets from me?" he spat, his words dripping with malice. "You think you can hide your past?"

I shrank away, but his anger was unstoppable. He hurled the whiskey bottle against the wall, the glass shattering into a hundred pieces.

My world crumbled as his cruelty unleashed itself upon me. The memories of Karthik, once a source of strength, now only fueled Vittal's rage.

He slapped me hard—so hard that my vision blurred for a moment, and a sharp sting spread across my cheek. The shock of the first blow hadn't even settled when another came, and then another, each one fiercer than the last. My head snapped to the side with the force, the metallic taste of blood filling my mouth as my lip split open.

Each slap echoed in the silence of the room, a deafening reminder of his power and my vulnerability. I could barely keep my footing, swaying under the assault as my world spun in disorienting circles.

My ears rang with the impact, but I could still hear his voice—harsh, venomous, filled with a rage that I didn't fully understand. His words cut deeper than the strikes, each syllable a dagger aimed straight at my spirit.

I raised a trembling hand to shield my face, but it was futile. He swatted it away with ease, his strength overwhelming mine. The sharp, rhythmic cracks of his palm against my skin continued, each one punctuating the endless loop of fear and submission that had become my life.

Tears spilled down my cheeks unbidden, mingling with the blood that now trickled from the corner of my mouth. My body recoiled with every blow, but there was nowhere to run, nowhere to hide.

With every slap, a silent scream built up inside me, pressing against the walls of my chest. I wanted to cry out, to fight back, to demand that he stop, but the words choked in my throat. Fear silenced me, as it always did, its heavy chains wrapping tighter around my soul.

Just when I thought it was over, his grip tightened painfully. "You'll never forget Karthik again," he hissed. "You'll never forget what belongs to me."You're mine," he growled, his fingers digging into my skin. "Your past, your present, your future—everything belongs to me."

My pleas fell on deaf ears as his alcohol-fueled fury consumed him. My body trembled, my heart shattering into a million pieces under the weight of his wrath.

He was completely on me, a crushing weight that pinned me down in more ways than one. His disregard for my condition—my pregnancy—was an added cruelty, a stark reminder of how little my voice and my well-being mattered to him. I pleaded with my eyes, whispered weak protests, but he ignored them all, his actions fueled by an insatiable desire to dominate, to control.

Each second felt like an eternity as he pushed harder, deeper, and deeper into his own selfish need, oblivious to my cries or the fragility of my body. My swollen abdomen ached with a sharp intensity that made me tremble, but I lacked the strength to fight back. Every ounce of energy had already been drained from me, leaving me helpless beneath his weight.

I tried to push him off, feebly attempting to shove against the broad, immovable force pinning me down. But my arms, trembling with weakness and exhaustion, gave way almost instantly. I couldn't summon the strength to fight, and the reality of my powerlessness gnawed at my spirit.

The pain was unbearable, both physical and emotional—a searing agony that consumed every inch of my being. My body was stretched to its limits, my mind racing with fear and desperation. I felt my spirit begin to crumble, piece by piece, as his actions reduced me to something less than human, less than whole.

And then, amidst the turmoil, a singular, haunting thought emerged, silencing everything else. It was cold, stark, and unrelenting: This is what my life has become. This is all I am now.

Tears streamed silently down my face, merging with the waves of despair that coursed through me. It wasn't just the physical pain—it was the suffocating realization of how utterly trapped I was. The walls around me, both literal and figurative, seemed to close in tighter, squeezing out any remnants of hope or resistance.

In that moment, something inside me broke, but it wasn't defeat—it was the shattering of an illusion. The illusion that if I endured enough, things might change. That if I suffered quietly, he might one day see my pain and stop. But that moment never came, and the breaking of my spirit became the first step toward the realization that I couldn't stay like this.

This wasn't living—it was surviving, barely holding on. And as the tears dried on my cheeks, replaced by a cold resolve, a new thought emerged, fragile but defiant: This cannot be my end.

Escape.

I knew it wouldn't be easy. Vittal's control was suffocating, but I had to try. For myself, for my child, and for the memories I held dear.

The dawn finally broke, casting faint light on the shattered remains of my world. Vittal's anger had burned itself out, leaving a chilling calm in its wake.

I lay still, bruised in body and heavy in heart, yet somewhere within me, a flicker of resolve remained.

XII

A Plan

Morning light crept cautiously through the window, casting a pale glow across my swollen cheek and bruised arms. I lay there for a moment, staring at the ceiling, dreading the hours ahead. But beneath the pain and exhaustion, there was something new, something that hadn't been there before: a fresh resolve. I had learned to hide it well, but my heart beat a steady rhythm of quiet defiance. The fear was still there, lurking, but it no longer held me the way it once had. Not anymore.

The sound of footsteps broke the stillness, and before I could brace myself, Vittal's mother appeared at the doorway, her shadow casting long and cold across the room. She never offered any sympathy, never any understanding. Her face was hard, as immovable as the ancient wooden pillars that held up this house. "Satya," she barked, her tone clipped, "Get up. Don't think your condition gives you any right to laze around. There is work to be done."

I winced at her words, at the pain that surged through my body as I pushed myself up. Every muscle screamed in protest, but I wouldn't let myself show weakness—not in front of her, not in front of anyone. She was always watching, waiting for the slightest sign of vulnerability. To give her that satisfaction would be to allow her to strip away what little dignity I had left.

The day dragged on in its relentless, mechanical rhythm. Chores piled on top of each other, each one a reminder of my prison. Scrubbing the floors until my hands were raw, cooking elaborate meals that no one truly appreciated, washing clothes by hand as my arms trembled under the weight of it all—every task was a reminder of just how small and powerless I had become in their eyes. My mother-in-law hovered like a vulture, her gaze sharp, dissecting every move I made, criticizing even the slightest deviation from her rigid standards. I knew I had to endure it. I had no choice.

But the worst pressure didn't come from her, nor even from Vittal. No, the worst came from his father. His demands were subtle, but insistent. "A boy will bring prosperity to our family," he would say, his voice heavy with expectation as he peered at me from across the breakfast table. "A son will secure our lineage." His words were not meant to uplift but to burden. To reduce me to nothing more than a vessel for his desires.

And his voice would thunder from the living room, each word dripping with expectation. "Remember, Satya, this family expects a male heir. Don't forget the burden you carry. A boy will be the pride of this family, and you had better do everything in your power to ensure it."

I could feel the weight of those words pressing down on my chest, suffocating me. In their eyes, I wasn't a person. I wasn't a woman. I was a tool, a symbol. My child, the one growing inside me, wasn't a life—he was merely an asset to further their legacy. I clenched my fists, my nails digging into my palms, angry but controlled. No. They would never control my child the way they controlled me.

But there was something else that haunted me. A threat, dark and venomous, that Vittal had whispered into my ear the night before. His words slithered into my mind, cold and calculating, like a snake ready to strike. "You'll learn to obey," he had said, his voice low and threatening. "You'll forget your past, your spirit, everything. And if you think you can defy me, think again."

His words had been like chains, invisible but unbreakable, wrapping themselves around my chest, squeezing the breath from me. But if he thought he could break me, he was wrong. I would submit outwardly, yes, I would play the part, but inside, I was building walls. Walls to shield the flickering flame of hope that still burned inside me. For the sake of my child, I would not allow him to extinguish it.

As the day wore on, I began to formulate a plan. A quiet rebellion. I had to be careful, patient. I needed to endure the malice from Vittal, the constant surveillance from my mother-in-law, and the relentless pressure from my father-in-law. But with each passing hour, I was becoming sharper, more alert, attuned to the rhythms of the household, the cracks in their carefully constructed world.

That afternoon, when the house fell into a rare moment of quiet—Vittal's mother had gone to the market, and his father was resting—I saw an opportunity. A fleeting moment of solitude.

I tiptoed toward the small room I had transformed into a makeshift nursery. It was modest, nothing compared to the grand rooms in the rest of the house, but it was mine. I placed my hand gently over my belly, feeling the faint flutter of life inside me. My heart swelled with love and determination. "Don't worry, my child," I whispered softly. "We'll get out of here. One day, you'll see the world beyond these walls. A world where you'll be free."

Just as I exhaled, I heard a creak from the hallway. My heart stopped in my chest, and I froze, listening intently. Had someone heard me? Was someone outside the door? But then, I realized it was just the draft. I let out a breath of relief, but I knew this moment of solitude wouldn't last. I would have to be more careful, more vigilant.

From that moment, I became a ghost in this house, moving through the rooms like a shadow. I was the obedient wife, the dutiful daughter-in-law, but beneath the surface, I was a silent storm, gathering strength. I memorized the patterns of their lives—the time Vittal spent in the office, the moments my in-laws would retire to their rooms, the moments when the house was at its quietest. Every small detail became a piece of the puzzle I was slowly assembling.

Days passed, and Vittal grew more arrogant, his confidence in my submission swelling with every passing hour. He was blind to the quiet rebellion brewing beneath the surface. He thought his cruelty had broken me, but he couldn't have been more wrong. I played the part, yes, I bent to his will outwardly, but inside, I was building a life of my own. A life where I was no longer a victim, but a woman with a plan.

Then, one evening, as I served dinner, I overheard Vittal talking about a business trip he had planned. "I'll be heading to Mumbai for three days," he said, his tone full of self-importance. My pulse quickened at the mention of those three days. Three days—just a small window of time. But it was all I needed. The chance I had been waiting for.

I waited until the conversation was over, nodding along as though I were nothing more than the obedient wife he thought me to be. But inside, my mind was already racing, making preparations.

That night, after everyone had retired to their rooms, I crept into the kitchen, my heart pounding in my chest. I wrote a note, hurried and desperate, slipping it into the small pouch I had been secretly keeping hidden in my clothing. It felt like a lifeline—a declaration of my intent. Tomorrow would be the day. The only chance I had to escape this life.

As I cleared the table, I could feel my mother-in-law's critical gaze on me. But I didn't flinch. I didn't show any sign of the fear that was curling inside my stomach. I smiled, as though nothing was wrong. But behind my eyes, a fierce vow burned: "I will escape. I will protect my child."

That night, as I lay in bed, my hand rested protectively over my belly. Tomorrow would be the start of something new. A journey toward freedom. I whispered to my child, my voice barely audible, "Tomorrow, we begin our journey to freedom." And with that vow, I closed my eyes, knowing that no matter what, I would find a way out. I would give my child the life they deserved. And I would be free.

XIII

Guest

I woke with a start, my heart pounding in my chest. Today was the day. For weeks, I had been planning every detail, every move, every step to escape. The moment I had longed for had finally arrived. Vittal was gone, off on his business trip, and I had three full days of freedom—three days to break free from this prison I had been caged in. My bag was packed, my note hidden carefully in my clothing, and my resolve was as firm as steel.

But as I swung my legs over the side of the bed, ready to set my plan into motion, the shrill sound of the doorbell sliced through the air. My breath caught in my throat. Who could that be? I wasn't expecting anyone. The fragile bubble of my plans seemed to burst in an instant, replaced by an icy dread.

I froze for a moment, trying to steady my racing pulse. Was it possible that someone had discovered my plan? Had I made a mistake? My mind spun with wild thoughts as I hurried to the window, trying to get a glimpse of the visitor and then I saw her.

Meena.

Of course, it had to be her.

Vittal's sister, always so lively, so smug, standing at the front door with a wide grin plastered on her face. She waved, her smile too bright, her manner too cheery. Behind her, two children—Vittal's niece and nephew—tugged at her sleeves, eager to enter the house. Their luggage was piled high beside her.

I felt the air leave my lungs. This wasn't good. This couldn't be happening.

Had Vittal sent her to check on me? To make sure I was "staying in my place"? My heart skipped a beat as panic clawed at my throat. No, it wasn't just that. Meena had always been a problem. She was sharp, calculating, and above all, she took pleasure in knowing she could stir chaos.

I opened the door slowly, forcing a smile that felt brittle, as if it might crack the moment she looked too closely. "Meena," I said, trying to sound as warm as I could manage. "What a surprise. What brings you here?"

Her eyes sparkled with that annoying enthusiasm of hers, as if nothing could ever be wrong in her world. "I thought I'd come stay for a few days!" she announced, stepping past me as though she had every right to be here. "The kids need a little break from school, and I thought it would be nice to spend some time together. You and I can catch up!" She breezed past me as though she owned the place, and the children ran in after her, their laughter bouncing off the walls.

I stood frozen in the doorway, my mind racing. This was a disaster. How could I possibly escape now with her here, hovering over me, always so keenly aware of my every move? She would never let me leave unnoticed.

I tried to steady my breath, but the anxiety clawed at me. I had worked so hard to get to this point, so close to breaking free, only to have her show up like this. Meena didn't just visit; she dominated. She would turn my world upside down if given the chance—and she would never let me get away with anything. Not without some sort of game, some twisted manipulation.

As she began unpacking, my mind spun with the realization of just how difficult this would be. Meena wasn't just here to "catch up"—she was here to observe, to control, and to make sure that I stayed exactly where I belonged: under her watchful eye, under her scrutiny.

The sound of her children running through the house, playing with toys and exploring every corner, made my stomach twist. Every minute they were here, I was losing precious time. Time that I couldn't afford to waste. And what made it worse was that Meena was the one who would notice the smallest change in the air—the slightest hint of something being off.

"Satya," Meena called from the other room, her voice sharp and insistent. "Are you alright? You seem a little... distracted. Something on your mind?"

I forced myself to turn, meeting her gaze. There was no way she hadn't noticed the tension in my body. She was too smart, too calculating for that and worse, she enjoyed it.

"Oh, I'm just a bit tired," I lied, trying to make my voice sound light and unaffected. "It's nothing, really. I'm just glad you're here. It's been a while since we spent time together." I smiled, though it felt like the words were cutting my tongue.

She didn't buy it. I could see the flicker of suspicion in her eyes as she leaned in slightly, scrutinizing me with that unsettling gaze. "You sure? You've been looking a little worn down lately. Vittal's been hard on you, hasn't he?" Her tone was casual, but the words, the question itself, felt like a trap.

I swallowed, my heart pounding, but I forced myself to nod. "Yes, just a bit tired from the usual work. But it's nice to have you here, Meena. Really."

She seemed satisfied with the answer, but the way she lingered in the doorway, watching me, made my skin crawl. Meena wasn't just here to visit. She was here to make sure I stayed in my place. She had always enjoyed putting me under her thumb, making me feel small and insignificant in her presence. Now, with her here, I felt like I was back in that cage I had fought so hard to escape from.

ꕥ

As the evening wore on, I could feel the walls closing in on me. Every word she spoke was laced with something I couldn't quite pin down. It was like she was toying with me, prodding me with questions, waiting for me to slip up, waiting for me to show even the slightest sign of rebellion.

Meena wasn't just a harmless guest. She was a predator, and I was her prey.

Her children went to bed, leaving the house still and quiet, but the tension between Meena and me grew thick in the air. She leaned forward across the dinner table, her eyes narrowing. "You know," she began, her voice low but sharp, "I've been thinking... You seem so different lately. I can't quite put my finger on it, but something's changed. Is there something you're not telling me, Satya?"

I froze, my heart leaping into my throat. She was getting too close to the truth. She knew something was off. She just didn't know what. Yet.

I swallowed hard, the words nearly choking me. "No, Meena," I said, my voice shaky. "Everything's fine. Really." I forced another smile, but it felt like a mask that might slip at any moment.

She studied me for a long moment, and I could see the wheels turning in her mind. She knew. She knew something was wrong. The question was, would she figure it out before I could leave?

That night, as I lay in bed, my hand resting protectively over my belly, I felt the weight of her presence bearing down on me. Meena was no longer just a nuisance; she had become a threat. The small window of freedom I had fought for was closing fast, and if I didn't act quickly, she would be the one to trap me here for good.

I had no choice now. I would have to play her game, pretending that nothing had changed. I would have to deceive her, manipulate her, just as she had done to me for all these years.

The plan had to change. But I wasn't backing down. I couldn't. For my child. For my freedom.

ꕥ

Meena's presence suffocated me. It was like a thick, oppressive cloud that hovered over every corner of the house, following me even into the quietest spaces. She was always there—watching, questioning, controlling. Every time I thought I could steal a moment of respite, she would appear, demanding more of me, imposing herself in ways both subtle and blatant.

Her children—wild, unruly, never disciplined—raced through the house, screaming, knocking things over, and leaving a trail of chaos behind them. And yet, Meena did nothing to stop them. She didn't raise a finger to guide them, to quiet them, to ensure that the house remained in any semblance of order. Instead, she dumped the responsibility of caring for them onto me, as if I were her personal servant.

"Satya, can you make sure the kids eat their lunch?" she would ask lazily from the couch, her fingers lazily scrolling through her phone, as if I didn't have enough to do. She never even glanced up from her screen, too comfortable in her own world, too entitled to consider that I might have my own needs.

"Satya, can you help Charan with his homework?" she'd call, her voice distant, disinterested, as though it were my job to parent her children. Her gaze remained fixed on whatever triviality held her attention at the moment, oblivious to the fact that I was struggling just to keep up with the demands of the household, let alone the fatigue pulling at my body with each passing day.

I tried to comply, I had to comply. If I didn't, the sharpness of her criticism would come, her pointed remarks turning into silent judgments, a heavy weight that pressed down on me. But each time I did, I felt my strength—my resolve—drain a little more. The constant demands took their toll. My pregnancy, once a source of quiet joy, now felt like an endless burden. The exhaustion, the aches in my back, the weariness that gnawed at my bones—it all intensified as I pushed myself harder and harder to meet her needs. But Meena, of course, didn't care. She never saw the toll it was taking on me.

One evening, as I was preparing dinner—my back aching, my stomach rolling with discomfort—Meena sauntered into the kitchen, all self-assuredness and smugness, her gaze sweeping over the pots and pans.

"Let me show you how it's done," she said, her voice dripping with condescension. "You're doing it all wrong."

I bit back the retort that burned at the back of my throat. There was no use in anger; it would only fuel her needling, her sharp tongue. Instead, I stood there, hands frozen in place, seething silently. She took the spoon from my hand, as though I were too inept to cook for my own family. The sharp clatter of the spoon against the pot echoed in my mind, her every word cutting deeper than the last.

She went on, criticizing everything—how I had chopped the vegetables, how the spices weren't right, how I had let the pot simmer for too long. Her children, who had been frolicking in the other room, now stood by the door, wide-eyed, watching the spectacle unfold. They too seemed to take pleasure in the way she tore me down. Meena's presence had become a performance—her dominance over me, a public spectacle for her children, a reminder of just how far beneath her I was.

The evening passed in a haze of frustration. Every movement felt like an effort, every task a reminder of my own helplessness. The pain in my body was only heightened by the constant demands of Meena's unrelenting presence. When the day finally ended, and I sank into bed, I felt a wave of despair wash over me.

Meena's touch was everywhere. I could feel it even in the stillness of the night. She had taken over my life, my space, my very soul. She had embedded herself into every corner of this house, into my every thought. The walls were closing in, and I was helpless to stop her.

XIV

Worse

The next morning, I awoke to her again, her eyes gleaming with that smug sense of superiority that seemed to fuel her every action. I could feel her watching me as I stumbled into the living room, my body already protesting the movement.

"Satya," she said, as if she had been waiting for me to appear. "I've been thinking..." She paused, her gaze narrowing with calculated malice. "You need to start taking care of yourself. You're looking a bit... unkempt."

I forced a smile, but inside, I felt a seething tide of anger rising. How dare she—how dare she—critique my appearance, especially when she had done nothing but add to my burden? I was barely holding it together, my body battered by her demands, my mind fraying at the edges, and yet, she had the gall to suggest that I wasn't taking care of myself?

"I'm fine, Meena," I replied, my voice tight, barely keeping it together. "Just a bit tired."

But she wouldn't let it go. Her eyes glinted with that familiar, patronizing gleam, and before I could blink, she was up, walking toward me with an air of authority, as though she could control every aspect of my life.

"No, no," she insisted, dismissing my words. "I can see it. You're not taking care of yourself at all. Let me help."

With that, she began to dictate every small detail of my life. From the clothes I wore to the food I ate. "You need to eat more vegetables," she'd say, handing me plates of food that I didn't want, as if I couldn't make my own choices. "You shouldn't wear that dress, it makes you look older," she'd tell me, picking out something more appropriate—more to her liking, of course.

It wasn't just the physical demands that were draining me, it was the humiliation, the way she turned every gesture, every action, into a statement of my inadequacy. She didn't just want me to serve her; she wanted me to be less than her—she wanted me to disappear into the shadows of her life, to be nothing but a reflection of what she decided I should be.

I felt like a prisoner in my own home, but the bars weren't made of iron. They were made of her constant interference, her insistence on shaping me into something I wasn't, and could never be.

Vittal's control was suffocating, but Meena's was worse. Her presence didn't just confine me; it humiliated me. Every word she spoke, every look she gave, reinforced the idea that I was nothing. That I would never be anything more than her servant, her plaything.

As the days blurred together, I realized something: I couldn't let this continue. I couldn't let her destroy what little hope I had left. My chance at freedom was slipping away, and I had to outsmart her. I couldn't let her see the cracks forming inside me, not yet. I had to keep playing her game, pretending to be the submissive, obedient wife she expected.

But deep inside, I was burning with rage. Each act of compliance, each moment of silent endurance, only added to my resolve. Meena was pushing me closer to the edge, but little did she know, every harsh word, every judgment, every piece of control she took from me, only fueled my determination.

I would escape. And when I did, I would leave her, Vittal, and their toxic games behind forever.

ꕤ

The clock was ticking. The plan was still in motion. And Meena? She was about to learn just how dangerous a woman backed into a corner can be.

As I stood in the dimly lit kitchen, Meena's sharp instructions filled the air like an endless, relentless hum. She was relentless, hovering over my shoulder, her voice biting and critical as she dictated each step, as though I were an incompetent child. Her words stung, but I bit my tongue and continued. The desperate feeling clawed at my heart, intensifying with each of her commands. Vittal would be home in two days. I could already feel the weight of his presence, the thick, oppressive air that settled in the house whenever he returned. His arrival would embolden Meena further, amplifying her harshness, and I would be trapped between them—two forces determined to control and break me.

The thought alone sent a shiver down my spine. I couldn't let that happen, not when I had come so close to my quiet resistance, so close to my plan for freedom. But until the moment came, I had to endure. So I continued to scrub, to clean, to cook, bearing the weight of my exhaustion and hiding my bruises as best I could.

The family's indifference to my condition was unshakable. They ignored my pale face, my trembling hands, and the fatigue that weighed down my every step. At six months pregnant, I should have been resting, nurturing this fragile life within me, but no one seemed to care. Meena piled chores on me as if I were her personal servant, and Vittal's parents were content to turn a blind eye. They had their own rigid beliefs, their own definitions of strength, and to them, my struggles were simply proof of my inadequacy.

One afternoon, my body could take no more. I felt a wave of dizziness sweep over me, and before I knew it, I was on the floor, the hard tiles pressing against my cheek as the world spun around me. I reached out instinctively, searching for something to hold on to, but only emptiness met my hands. My pulse thundered in my ears, and nausea twisted my stomach as I fought to steady myself.

Meena's footsteps pounded across the kitchen floor as she appeared over me, her face twisted in irritation rather than concern. "What are you doing on the floor, Satya?" she snapped, crossing her arms. "Stop being so dramatic. We all have work to do."

I struggled to sit up, each movement sending jolts of pain through my limbs. I managed to stammer, "I... I just felt dizzy..."

Her expression didn't soften. If anything, her impatience only deepened. "You're pregnant, not dying," she said coldly. "A little dizziness is nothing. You need to toughen up. You'll be a mother soon, and you can't go fainting at every little inconvenience."

She didn't offer me a hand. Instead, she turned and walked away, leaving me to pull myself up off the floor alone. I wanted to scream, to tell her that I wasn't being dramatic, that I was exhausted and terrified, that I was human. But I knew it would make no difference. In her eyes, I was weak, incapable. She dismissed my struggles as an inconvenience, something she could scold and ignore.

Desperation pushed me to take matters into my own hands. I started hiding painkillers and vitamins in my clothes, sneaking them into my room. Each night, as quietly as I could, I swallowed them in the dark, hoping they would dull the aches and keep me steady. I knew it wasn't ideal—there was a deep fear gnawing at me, a fear that I might harm my unborn child, but what choice did I have? Meena's gaze was everywhere, always watching, and I couldn't risk her finding out.

The thought of reaching out to my parents often crossed my mind. In quiet moments, I imagined their voices, imagined telling them everything, hearing the comfort and love that had once wrapped around me like a shield. I knew what they would say: "Leave him, Satya. Come home. We'll take care of you." And in my heart, I yearned for that safety. I ached for the warmth of my childhood home, for my mother's gentle hands and my father's reassuring smile. I longed to be somewhere where I wasn't reduced to a mere possession, where I wasn't constantly reminded of my supposed inadequacies.

But it wasn't that simple. Vittal's grip on me was complex, tangled in layers of loyalty, fear, and the weight of his family's influence. There was a twisted sense of ownership that he held over me, a belief that I was his to control, to mold to his whims. He wasn't just my husband; he was a powerful figure in his family, a man with a web of connections that could stretch far beyond my reach. Leaving him wasn't simply walking out of a door—it was a leap into an unknown darkness, one where I might be followed, where I might be found and dragged back.

And yet, the flicker of hope inside me wouldn't be extinguished. I knew I had to do this on my own, to find my way out, for myself and for the child I was carrying. It wasn't just about survival anymore—it was about freedom, about building a life where my child and I wouldn't live in fear. Each day, I held on to that dream, nurturing it in the quiet corners of my heart, letting it fill me with strength I hadn't known I possessed.

The days blurred together in a haze of exhaustion and desperation, my small acts of rebellion hidden beneath layers of submission. As the sun set each evening, casting long shadows across the walls, I would whisper to my child, "One day, we will be free. I promise you that." And though the promise felt distant, as elusive as smoke in the wind, it gave me something to hold onto, a reason to keep going.

As Vittal's return loomed closer, my anxiety sharpened, each heartbeat a reminder of the time ticking away. I felt the weight of his presence even before he arrived, as if his shadow had already settled over the house, darkening every corner. But this time, I was prepared. I had endured their taunts, their cold indifference, and their relentless expectations. I had borne the weight of Meena's scorn and Vittal's control, and now I was ready to reclaim what little control I had left.

I knew my chance was coming, and when it did, I would be ready. I would fight, I would resist, and I would break free. For myself, for my child, and for the future that we both deserved. The world outside might have forgotten me, but I hadn't forgotten myself. Beneath the layers of obedience and endurance, I was still here—fierce, unbroken, and quietly planning my escape.

XV

Toxic

The doorbell rang, a sharp, jarring sound that sliced through the already tense silence of the house. Meena's face lit up as she hurried to answer it, her features softening in a way that they never did with me. Vittal's cousins—Viswam and Sampath—stood in the doorway, grinning broadly as they stepped into the house with an air of entitlement that made my skin crawl.

"Ah, Viswam! Sampath! Come in, come in!" Meena greeted them with a warmth she never afforded anyone else, enveloping them in a warm embrace before guiding them into the living room. Their loud voices filled the house, brimming with confidence and arrogance, as if they owned the very walls that surrounded us.

I remained in the kitchen, trying to focus on preparing their meal, my fingers clumsy as I chopped vegetables. But my heart wasn't in it. My heart was pounding in my chest, each beat a reminder that I was about to spend the evening with these strangers, forced to play the role of the perfect, obedient wife under Meena's watchful eye. I felt a sinking dread as I realized this evening would be no different from the countless others spent tiptoeing through their demands and expectations.

Just as I focused on slicing a carrot, I sensed someone entering the kitchen. I looked up to see Sampath standing there, watching me with an unsettling intensity. His gaze was heavy, predatory, like a lion sizing up its prey, and I felt a chill crawl up my spine as his eyes roamed over me, lingering on my pregnant belly with a twisted fascination.

"Satya, isn't it?" he asked, his voice smooth but with a dark undertone that hinted at something sinister.

I nodded, managing a polite, forced smile. "Yes, that's right."

Sampath's eyes didn't move from me. He smirked, and the corners of his mouth curled in a way that turned his face into something cruel, almost mocking. "You're looking... well," he said, his words dripping with sarcasm and insincerity.

I glanced down, busying myself with the vegetables, desperately wishing he would leave. But he didn't. Instead, he stepped closer, his presence filling the small kitchen, suffocating me with an air that reeked of malice. Leaning in, he whispered in my ear, his breath hot against my skin. "I hear you're quite the obedient wife. Vittal's lucky to have someone so... compliant."

I spun around, instinctively backing away to create space between us, but he closed the gap again in an instant. His hand shot out, fingers wrapping around my wrist with a vice-like grip, holding me in place. Panic surged through me as I looked up, meeting his gaze, and saw the cruel amusement dancing in his eyes.

"Let go," I whispered, my voice shaking but laced with defiance as I tried to yank my hand free.

"Oh, I'm sorry," he said with a mocking chuckle, his hand loosening but not entirely releasing me. "I didn't mean to frighten you, Satya."

Finally, he let go, stepping back with a smirk, clearly enjoying the discomfort he had inflicted. I watched him saunter out of the kitchen, leaving behind a trail of fear that seeped into every corner. My heart was racing, my thoughts tangled in fear and anger. I could still feel the lingering touch of his hand on my wrist, a phantom reminder of his cruel, invasive presence.

As I shakily prepared the rest of the meal, I kept replaying the encounter in my mind. This wasn't harmless flirtation—it was a power play, a twisted show of dominance meant to put me in my place. And the worst part was, I couldn't do a thing about it. In this household, I was nothing more than a silent, invisible presence, an object to be controlled, judged, and dismissed.

Dinner was a tense affair. Meena had orchestrated a lavish spread, filling the table with dishes I'd painstakingly prepared under her meticulous watch. Viswam and Sampath took their seats, exchanging loud jokes and laughter with Vittal, who seemed to revel in their company. Their conversation filled the room, an unending stream of stories and crude jokes, masking the underlying darkness that simmered just below the surface. Sampath's eyes continued to find mine across the table, a flicker of amusement flashing in them whenever he caught me looking his way. Each glance made my skin crawl, as though I were under a microscope, laid bare for his twisted amusement.

Meena's gaze never left me, her sharp eyes noting every movement, every expression. Her silent but fierce scrutiny made it clear—any hint of rebellion, any refusal to play my role would not be tolerated. She expected me to smile, to serve, to remain silent, and I complied, hiding my unease and rage behind a mask of submission. But with each passing second, the suffocating weight of it all pressed down harder, like invisible chains tightening around my chest.

After what felt like an eternity, the meal finally drew to a close. Viswam and Sampath stood up, their boisterous laughter filling the room as they prepared to leave. Sampath threw one last look my way, his lips curling into a smirk that hinted at secrets I didn't want to imagine. He knew exactly what he was doing—he'd planted a seed of fear, and he wanted me to know it would grow.

As they walked out the door, Meena turned to me, her expression cold, her lips pressed into a thin, satisfied line. "You did well tonight, Satya," she said, her voice filled with a biting edge. "But don't think you're safe. You're still mine to command." Her words hung heavy in the air, a reminder of her hold over me, a reminder that this house was her domain, and I was nothing but a pawn in her game.

I bit back the angry retort rising in my throat, swallowing it down like a bitter pill as I moved to clear the table. My hands shook, the dishes rattling as I stacked them, but I forced myself to maintain control. I wouldn't give her the satisfaction of seeing me falter.

The moment I was alone in the kitchen, I leaned against the counter, my body trembling as the fear and anger I'd held back surged to the surface. Sampath's visit had awakened a new terror, a realization that Vittal's cruelty was not contained to just him but extended to his entire family. His cousins were just as toxic, just as eager to exert control, to belittle and dominate.

And yet, despite the fear that gripped me, a spark of defiance burned within. I couldn't let them break me. I couldn't let Sampath's threats, Vittal's coldness, or Meena's cruelty push me to the edge. I had a promise to keep—to myself, and to the child growing inside me. A promise that, one day, we would be free of this place, free from these people who tried to own and control us.

As I finished cleaning up, I whispered to myself in the quiet of the kitchen, "One day, this will all be over. One day, I will be free." And with that thought, I held on, the small flame of hope inside me growing a little brighter, ready to face whatever darkness came next.

ꟷ

The days seemed to blur together, one agonizing moment blending into the next, creating a haze of dread that hung over me like a storm cloud. Each day felt like an endless cycle of serving, silence, and subjugation, with no escape in sight. Vittal's cousins, Viswam and Sampath, had taken to visiting frequently, filling the house with their laughter and veiled threats, amplifying the fear that already gnawed at me. Their presence had become a twisted routine, one more knot in the toxic web that I was ensnared in, my life entangled with people who saw me as little more than an object.

One evening, as the sun began to sink below the horizon, I opened the door to Mr. Rao, Vittal's father. He stood there, his gaze lingering on me in a way that sent an immediate shiver down my spine. I felt a sharp sense of unease settle into the pit of my stomach as I greeted him. But before I could step aside to let him in, he reached out and grasped my hand, his fingers digging into my skin with an unsettling familiarity.

"Satya, my dear," he murmured, his voice a sickly-sweet blend of affection and malice, "you're looking lovely today."

I tried to pull away, to create some distance, but his grip only tightened, and the look in his eyes grew darker. He leaned in closer, close enough that I could feel his breath, and I was struck by a suffocating wave of disgust as I saw his other hand moving in a way that made my stomach twist. He was pleasuring himself, his eyes fixed on mine as if daring me to react, to scream, to recoil.

I stood there, rooted in shock and disbelief, my mind racing in a thousand directions but unable to process what was happening. Meena stood just behind him, watching the scene unfold with an impassive expression, her face a mask of cold indifference. She made no move to stop him, no effort to acknowledge my horror. Her silence was a betrayal that shattered any remnants of respect or trust I might have held for her.

Mr. Rao finally released my hand, stepping back with a satisfied smile that turned my stomach. "I'll see you inside," he said, his voice dripping with a smug satisfaction that sent a surge of anger and helplessness through me.

As he disappeared into the house, I stumbled back, trying to regain my composure, but the encounter had left me shaken to my core. How could they do this to me? How could they treat me like this in my own home, in the place that was supposed to be a sanctuary?

Meena's voice cut through the suffocating silence, cold and dismissive. "Satya, don't look so disturbed. It's just a harmless gesture."

Her words struck me like a slap. Harmless? Did she truly believe that, or was she merely condoning this vile behavior? I looked at her, searching for any trace of empathy, but found none. Her expression was indifferent, almost bored, as if this violation was no more than a mild inconvenience.

Without a word, I turned and retreated into the kitchen, my anger simmering beneath the surface. Mechanically, I began preparing dinner, chopping and stirring with hands that trembled from the fury and fear battling within me. The humiliation of it all was overwhelming. Every part of me wanted to scream, to run, to break free from the chains that kept me here, trapped in this endless cycle of control and cruelty.

But as I prepared the evening meal, visions of escape danced in my mind. I imagined a world beyond these walls, a life free from Vittal's oppressive influence, from Meena's toxic demands, and from Mr. Rao's sickening touch. I imagined taking my child, my unborn child who depended on me for protection, and running far from this place, to somewhere safe, somewhere warm and bright. But each time I considered it, the weight of my reality pressed down on me. Where would I go? Who would help me? And how could I protect my child if I failed?

The dining room that night was suffused with a tense, oppressive atmosphere. Mr. Rao sat at the head of the table, his presence darkening the air. Vittal attempted to laugh, forcing jokes and stories, but his words rang hollow. I went through the motions of serving and clearing, avoiding the eyes of everyone at the table, holding my emotions in a tight, quivering knot inside.

As the meal ended and Mr. Rao and the others drifted away, Meena's parting words echoed in my mind, a final twist of the knife. "Remember, Satya," she whispered, her voice as cold as ice, "you're ours. You'll do as you're told."

Every fiber of my being wanted to shout, to tell her that I would never belong to them, that I was not theirs to command. But I bit back the retort, pressing my lips together, forcing myself to remain silent. I knew I couldn't risk showing defiance—not yet. Not when I was still so vulnerable.

As I retreated to my room that night, her words haunted me, gnawing at my spirit, making me feel more trapped than ever before. But even in the depths of my despair, a flicker of hope glimmered within me. A voice, small but fierce, rose from somewhere deep inside.

One day, this will all be over. One day, I will break free from this toxic cycle. One day, I will reclaim my life.

That thought, that promise to myself and my child, was the only thing keeping me sane, the only thing that allowed me to close my eyes and drift into the restless, fractured sleep that awaited me. I held onto it like a lifeline, vowing that no matter how dark the days grew, I would not let them extinguish that fragile spark of hope.

XVI
Cruelty

The walls of Vittal's house had long felt like a prison, but now they seemed to close in tighter, suffocating me. Each passing day, the cruelty I endured grew more insidious, tearing at my spirit, testing my limits. I had always hoped that somehow things would improve, that the nightmare would ease. But I was wrong. Vittal's contempt had only grown sharper, his transgressions deeper.

One afternoon, while Vittal was out, I called my best friend, Maggi, the only person I knew I could trust. Speaking softly into the receiver, I poured out my heart. I told her everything – from the relentless torment by Vittal and his family to the indignities I suffered in silence. Each word, each painful truth I spoke, felt like ripping open a wound, and I broke down, sobbing uncontrollably.

Maggi's voice came through, soft yet fierce, a steadying presence in the storm of my emotions. "Satya, my dear, I had no idea... I'm so sorry. I can't imagine the strength it's taken for you to endure this." Her compassion steadied me, offering a warmth I hadn't felt in what felt like forever. "Listen, you're not alone," she continued. "I'll do everything

I can to help you. There's a way out, Satya. There has to be."

I could feel the warmth in her words, a steadying embrace over the phone.

"I know it's hard to see a path forward right now," she continued, "but we'll find one. You have options, even if it doesn't feel that way. Look, let's start with small steps. You've already taken the first one by talking to me, by opening up. And Satya, I'm here for you – whatever you need, whether it's someone to talk to or somewhere to stay. If you need to leave tonight, I'll drive over and get you. You and your baby deserve better, and I'll do everything I can to help you find a way."

Her words felt like a balm to my wounded spirit, soothing, yet stirring something inside me—a small glimmer of hope I hadn't felt in so long.

"Satya, I want you to start putting a few things aside, even if it's just a small bag hidden away. You don't have to leave right now, but you should feel prepared if things get worse. Do you have somewhere safe to keep important documents? Your ID, money, anything you need? I can help with whatever's missing."

"Yes," I replied, barely able to hold back more tears. I hadn't allowed myself to even think about taking such steps, but Maggi's calm confidence and practical ideas planted seeds of determination.

"Remember, Satya," she said, her voice fierce again, "No matter what he or his family tries to make you believe, none of this is your fault. None of it. The way they've treated you is their shame, not yours. You have nothing to be ashamed of, and everything to be proud of. Look at you – carrying a child, keeping your dignity, staying so strong through all of this."

Her words wrapped around me like a shield, giving me something solid to hold onto. For the first time, I felt a sliver of strength returning, fueled by Maggi's unwavering support.

Her words felt like a glimmer of light breaking through the darkness. But even as I clung to this newfound hope, I couldn't shake the feeling that worse was yet to come.

ည

As my pregnancy entered its eighth month, I became more vulnerable, and Vittal's cruelty escalated to a level that was beyond comprehension. One night, while I was resting, trying to keep my body and mind calm for the sake of my unborn child, Vittal returned home late. The murmur of voices outside our bedroom door stirred my uneasy sleep. Then, the door opened, and in walked Vittal—holding hands with Madhu.

My heart dropped, the scene before me both surreal and painfully real. Madhu glanced at me, her eyes filled with a triumphant, smug gleam as she clung to Vittal's arm, all but flaunting their relationship. They laughed together, the sound piercing through me like shards of glass. I couldn't hold back any longer; the hurt, the anger, the betrayal – it all surged forward, demanding release.

"How can you do this to me?" I shouted, my voice breaking.

Madhu smirked, her gaze cruel and unfeeling. She stepped closer, her tone venomous as she sneered, "Mind your own business, Satya." Without warning, she shoved me, her hand striking me hard enough to make me stumble.

The humiliation burned in my veins, each word Vittal spat searing my skin like fire. Rage pulsed through me, and before I could stop myself, my hand shot up and slapped her, the sharp crack echoing like thunder. But the satisfaction of that brief moment evaporated as Vittal's face contorted with fury. His arm swung before I could even brace myself, the force of his slap blinding me with pain as stars burst behind my eyes.

He grabbed a handful of my hair, dragging me across the floor, my body skidding painfully as I fought to keep up, stumbling and slipping, my knees scraping against the hard tiles. I cried out, my pleas catching in my throat, choked by a mix of pain and desperation, but my voice only seemed to fuel his cruelty.

"Get out," he snarled, his voice dripping with venom, each word a lash across my heart. He leaned in close, his face twisted in a cruel sneer. "You don't belong here. You're nothing but a burden—worthless."

With one final, violent shove, he threw me outside, sending me sprawling onto the unyielding concrete of the road. I fell hard, the force slamming into my stomach, and a scream tore from my throat as a searing pain shot through me. The dust settled around me, gritty and stinging, but all I could feel was the stabbing agony in my belly. I reached instinctively to protect my unborn child, cradling my stomach as the pain spread, sharp and merciless.

The pain shot through me, fierce and unforgiving, and I clutched my stomach instinctively, feeling a stab of terror as I realized something was terribly wrong. My baby... my mind screamed, but the words wouldn't come.

I staggered, trying to regain my balance, but the force of his push knocked me off my feet. I hit the ground hard, my body folding around my belly, a fresh wave of pain shooting through me. As I curled over in agony, I could feel my child inside me, the life I had nurtured, trembling with the shock that surged through us both.

A tearing pain sliced through me, and I doubled over, clutching my belly as my body curled in on itself. My heart raced, drowning out every other sound, every voice, every moment but this. The cold ground beneath me felt like iron, unyielding as my body shuddered with each new contraction, ripping through me with a force that stole my breath. I wanted to cry out, to scream for help, but the pain stole my voice, reducing my pleas to broken whispers.

In the distance, I could hear voices, footsteps, but they felt so far away. A small crowd gathered around me. I barely registered their faces, the looks of horror and pity in their eyes as they watched me, helpless and broken, fighting for both my life and my child's. Some of the neighborhood women knelt beside me, their hands gentle but firm, wiping the sweat from my brow, whispering words of encouragement as they urged me to push. I was grateful for their presence, yet I felt so alone, surrounded by strangers while the life I'd once trusted had turned against me.

I wanted to pull myself up, to find some shelter, but my body wouldn't obey. Instead, I felt the unmistakable, excruciating surge of labor pains. Not here, I thought, horror dawning on me as I realized I was going to give birth right there—on the filthy, unforgiving ground, with strangers staring, pity and disgust in their eyes. The humiliation of it clawed at me, almost as unbearable as the pain tearing through me.

As I struggled, gasping and writhing, I felt hands gently lifting me, voices murmuring soft words, offering a fragile lifeline of comfort. Neighbors, strangers—women who saw me, broken and bleeding, and still cared enough to help. Their kindness sliced through the haze of my despair, and I clung to their words, grounding myself in their strength."Breathe, you're not alone lady." one of them murmured, she looked at me with such kindness, it made the pain feel slightly more bearable.

The contractions came hard and fast, each one tearing through me, pushing me to the brink. I was lying in the dust, my clothes clinging to my blood-soaked skin, the gravel biting into my back. I wanted to scream at the injustice of it all—to think that I, a woman who had dreamed of a better life, was here, giving birth on a road like discarded refuse, exposed to the eyes of passing strangers.

The contractions came faster, relentless and unyielding, each wave of pain threatening to pull me under. I clung to the voices around me, the feel of their hands on my arms, and the warmth of their support as I fought to bring my child into a world that had shown me only cruelty.

My body pushed, each contraction wracking me with a fierce intensity that left me barely able to breathe. Finally, after what felt like an eternity of suffering, through the fog of agony, I heard the first cries of my child.—a small, delicate cry piercing through the silence. The sound filled my soul, a light in the darkness, and I felt a rush of love so intense it drowned out the pain. Someone gently placed her in my arms.

A GIRL, perfect and innocent, untouched by the hatred and suffering around us. As I looked at her, I felt a strength I'd never known surge within me. She was my reason to endure, my reason to live.

But as I held her tiny body close, exhaustion pulled at me, and the world began to fade. I wanted to fight it, to stay in this moment with her, to protect her from everything we'd just been through. But the pain and exhaustion were too strong, and my vision began to blur. The last thing I saw before the darkness took me was her tiny face, peaceful and pure, and I felt a flicker of hope. For her, I would rise again. For her, I would find the strength to break free.But the exhaustion was too much, the darkness pulling me under. I whispered to her, a quiet promise—"I will protect you." And with that, I surrendered to the shadows, knowing I had found a new strength, a reason to fight, and that one day, somehow, I would reclaim the life we both deserved.

As I slipped into unconsciousness, I felt the warmth of those around me, heard their voices murmuring in outrage and compassion, felt the gentle hand of a woman smoothing my hair, whispering softly that everything would be okay.

XVII

Safe

I sat beside Amma, adjusting the edge of my sari over my shoulder, I could feel the weight of her gaze on me, watching, worried. Her words felt familiar, almost rehearsed, but they still settled over me like a thick, stifling blanket.

"Satya," she began softly, her voice carrying that tone she reserved for moments she thought were important. "After marriage, you must always be patient and calm. Never shout at your husband, especially in front of his parents. You must fulfill your duties as a wife."

I lowered my eyes to my lap, fingers tracing over the cool metal of my wedding ring. I wanted to nod and say I understood, but a small part of me resisted. "But, Amma," I asked, hesitantly, "what if he... treats me unfairly? What if... he crosses a line?"

She sighed, looking almost disappointed that I'd asked. "It's natural to feel that way sometimes, Satya. But you mustn't react with anger or frustration. It's your duty to be patient, to bear it with grace. If your husband scolds you or even... even raises a hand, don't be harsh in return. Men... well, men have their tempers. But in time, he'll come around.so be silent.

Her words settled in my chest like a weight. "What if he doesn't understand, Amma? What if he never changes?"

She looked down, folding her hands tightly together. "Don't think like that, Satya. In time, if you're patient, if you're loyal, he'll see your goodness. Your endurance will earn his respect."

The word 'endurance' hung in the air, heavy and unyielding. "So I'm supposed to stay silent?" I whispered, almost to myself.

"Yes, my dear," she replied, her tone soft but firm. "By staying calm. Marriage is a commitment to sacrifice, to bearing more than you think you can. One day, he'll understand the depth of your loyalty, and that's how you win respect."

I wanted to ask her so much more — why should I have to stay silent if something feels wrong? Why can't I turn to anyone for help? But I bit my tongue, trying to accept what she was saying, even as it felt like my heart was resisting every word.

"Amma... if something feels truly wrong... can't I at least tell you?" I dared to ask, hoping she'd say yes, hoping she'd give me some thread of comfort.

But her face tightened, and she shook her head. "No, Satya. Never share your family life with outsiders. Not even me. Once you leave this house, your loyalty belongs there. Your duty is to protect your husband's honor — and your family's honor. No matter what."

The words were a blow. I couldn't stop the quiet "but..." that slipped out, my voice barely audible.

She reached out, cupping my cheek with a soft, weary expression. "I know, my child. I know it seems unfair. But I've seen more than you. I endured, and in the end, your father respected me for it. A woman's strength lies in her silence, Satya. You'll understand... one day."

I nodded, but my heart felt heavier than ever. I looked into her eyes, searching for some sign that maybe, once, she'd felt the same confusion I was feeling. That maybe, just maybe, she'd once longed for something different, too.

And deep down, as she continued to talk, a quiet, questioning whisper stirred within me — a sense that maybe, just maybe, there was another way to be strong.

ꟹ

It felt like waking from a dream — or maybe a nightmare I couldn't quite remember. My eyelids fluttered open, and a harsh, bright light from the hospital ceiling stung my eyes, making me squint as I struggled to focus. Disoriented, I lay still, piecing together fragments of memories, flashes of voices and faces. My mother's voice came to me then, her words lingering in my mind like a distant echo:

"Be patient, Satya. Be calm... endure, and one day he will understand."

The weight of those words sank heavily in my chest. How many times had I held on to that advice, hoping it would be enough? My throat tightened as memories resurfaced, along with the overwhelming pain and betrayal I had endured.

A soft, warm hand wrapped gently around mine, breaking my thoughts. I turned slightly and saw the kind face of a nurse watching me with concern, her voice soft and reassuring.

"Satya, welcome back. How are you feeling?"

I opened my mouth to speak, but my voice came out as a raspy whisper. "Where... where is my baby?" My throat felt parched, and each word seemed to scratch its way out.

The nurse's face softened into a gentle smile. "Your daughter is safe, Satya. She's in the nursery, and we'll bring her to you very soon. You've been through a lot, but you're safe now."

Safe.

The word lingered in the air, foreign yet comforting. Could it really be true? Images of my best friend Maggi flashed in my mind — her promise to help me find a way out. I had clung to her words in those dark days, hoping against hope that she could help me break free.

"Maggi?" I whispered, barely daring to believe.

The nurse nodded, her smile widening. "Your friend has been here the entire time, Satya. She's waiting right outside to see you. We'll let her in soon."

A sob escaped my lips, and tears slipped down my cheeks, each one a release, a small taste of the relief I had feared would never come. I wasn't alone. Not anymore.

And then, a sound pierced the quiet room, a soft, delicate cry, as if in answer to my heart's deepest longing. I turned, and the nurse appeared beside me, gently holding a tiny bundle wrapped snugly in a soft pink blanket. She bent down and placed the warm bundle in my arms, her voice a soothing murmur.

"Look who's here to meet her mommy," she said softly.

I looked down, and my breath caught in my throat. In my arms was the tiniest, most beautiful little face I'd ever seen, with soft cheeks and a delicate nose, her eyes squeezed shut as she squirmed slightly in my hold. She felt warm and fragile, and yet somehow, I felt that strength I had been searching for surge back into me.

"Hello, my darling," I whispered, my voice barely holding steady. Tears blurred my vision as I studied every detail of her face. "We're going to be okay. We're going to start over."

In that moment, all the suffering, the nights spent awake, the silent tears I had hidden for so long — it all felt like a shadow slipping away. All I could feel was this immense love for my daughter, the fierce need to protect her, to give her a life free from the darkness I had known.

Just then, the door opened softly, and Maggi walked in, her own eyes glistening with unshed tears. She came to my side, resting her hand on my shoulder, her voice filled with pride and emotion.

"Satya, you've come so far. I am so proud of you," she whispered, her face lighting up as she looked at my daughter. "You're free now, and you're so much stronger than you think."

I let out a shaky breath, absorbing her words. Free.

For the first time, the word didn't feel like a distant dream; it felt like a promise, one that had finally come true. I looked at my daughter, and then at Maggi, a quiet determination welling up inside me.

We would leave behind the shadows of the past, build a life of light and strength. I would find a way, not just for me, but for this tiny soul nestled in my arms, trusting me to give her a future as bright as the hope I felt now.

"Yes," I murmured, feeling the warmth of Maggi's hand steadying me, "we're free."

༄

My eyes drifted open, adjusting to the soft hospital light, and as they focused, I saw my parents standing nearby, their faces marked with worry and sadness. Ma's eyes, swollen and red from crying, met mine, and in that gaze, I saw the pain and regret she carried. She looked like she wanted to say something, but words failed her. Appa's face was lined with a kind of sorrow I hadn't seen before, his shoulders slumped, yet his arms opened wide as he came toward me.

"Satya, my child..." he whispered, his voice breaking. He wrapped his arms around me in a gentle hug, pulling me close as if trying to protect me from all the hurt I'd endured.

Ma joined, embracing us both, her tears falling freely as she held me tightly. "We're so sorry, Satya. We had no idea... we thought we were doing the right thing. We should have been there for you."

A lump formed in my throat as I hugged them back, feeling my own tears spill over. The tension, the anger, and the hurt I'd bottled up for so long started to dissolve in their embrace. "It's not your fault, Ma, Appa," I whispered, my voice trembling. "I didn't tell you... I didn't know how. I thought I could manage it on my own."

Appa's face crumpled with anguish, his fingers brushing a tear from my cheek. "We should have known, Satya. We should have looked for the signs. We should have been there to protect you." His regret was raw and real, and seeing it somehow brought me a strange sense of peace.

Maggi, who'd been standing quietly nearby, stepped back, letting us have this moment. My daughter stirred in my arms, her tiny hands wrapping around my finger, a gentle reminder that she was here with me, that she was safe.

Ma's voice was barely above a whisper as she spoke. "We thought we were doing what was best for you, Satya. We thought marriage would bring you happiness... and stability."

Looking into their remorseful eyes, I felt a mixture of forgiveness and understanding. "You did what you thought was right, Amma," I said gently. "But I've learned... I've learned that there's more to life than just enduring. There's strength in standing up, in speaking out, in asking for help."

Appa nodded, a tear slipping down his cheek. "You're right, Satya. And whatever you need now, we'll be here. We'll support you in every way."

We hugged again, this time with a sense of release. It was as if all the walls between us, all the misunderstandings and guilt, were finally breaking down. Forgiveness wrapped around us like a warm embrace, a soothing balm over the wounds that had hurt us all.

Maggi returned with a soft smile, sensing the peace that had settled in the room. "I think it's time I take care of some paperwork," she said, stepping out. "You all need some time together."

I turned to my parents, who were both watching me with a mixture of pride and sorrow. There was something I needed to tell them, a new hope I wanted to share. "Amma, Appa," I began, my voice steady and clear, "I have big dreams for my daughter's future. I want her to grow up strong and unafraid. I want her to know her worth, to speak up for herself. I want her to have a different life... a better life than I had."

Ma's eyes filled with hope, her hand resting on mine. "Oh, Satya, that's exactly what she deserves."

Appa's face set in determination as he held my other hand. "We'll do whatever it takes to help you give her that life. She'll grow up knowing how loved and precious she is."

As we held each other, tears of release mingling together, I felt a surge of newfound strength. I knew that from this moment on, I wasn't just a survivor; I was a mother with a purpose, a daughter who had reconciled with her parents, a woman ready to carve a new path for herself and her child. We were starting a new journey, one of healing, forgiveness, and rebirth, together.

XVIII

Regret

Days slipped by in a tense, quiet haze, each one marked by the conspicuous absence of Vittal's family. They didn't visit, didn't ask about my recovery, and most painfully, didn't care to see my daughter. Their disdain for her – simply because she was a girl – hung over me, but it only strengthened my resolve.

Maggi was at my side nearly every day, her face a mirror of the anger and frustration I felt. One afternoon, she looked at me with a fierce determination I had rarely seen. "Satya, this isn't right," she said, her voice barely containing the indignation. "You can't let them get away with this. After everything they put you through, you deserve justice."

I sighed, feeling the weight of her words. "I know, Maggi. But what can I do? They're powerful, and I'm just... I'm just me."

She shook her head, her hand reaching for mine, her grip firm. "You're stronger than you think, Satya. File a case. Report everything – the abuse, the neglect, the emotional torture."

Fear prickled up my spine, a familiar chill. "But Maggi... you know his family. His father has influence. They'd just silence me like they've silenced everyone else who ever dared to stand against them."

Maggi's hand tightened around mine, grounding me. "Not if we have the truth on our side. Not if we have evidence, Satya. You're not alone in this – you have people who care, who want to see you and your daughter safe."

I glanced at my parents. Amma's face was full of worry, her brow furrowed. "Satya," she said softly, her voice trembling. "We're scared for you. Vittal's father... he's a powerful man, and he has connections. We don't want to see you go through more pain."

Appa nodded in agreement, his jaw clenched with worry. "It's dangerous to go against him, and we don't want to lose you."

Their concern weighed heavily on me, but I knew deep down that I couldn't let fear keep me silent. I looked at them, a surge of courage rising in my chest. "I understand why you're worried. But if I stay silent, if I let them get away with this... they'll just keep hurting people. They'll keep thinking they can do whatever they want, with no consequences. I can't live with that."

Maggi gave my shoulder a gentle squeeze, her eyes shining with pride. "That's the Satya I know. Strong, unbreakable. They may think they've won, but they have no idea what you're capable of."

With Maggi's support and encouragement, I started gathering every piece of evidence I could. Hospital records, witness statements, documentation of the bruises and injuries I'd endured, anything that could help build a case. My parents, though nervous and still fearful, slowly began to come around. They stood by me as I organized everything, their love and quiet encouragement strengthening my resolve.

As we neared the day to file the case, I felt something shift inside me. I was no longer just surviving. I was fighting. I was claiming the power they had tried so hard to strip away. I was no longer just the victim; I was a survivor taking her first steps toward justice.

But Vittal's family wasn't going to let me go without a fight.

ꕥ

Satya stood by the window, the soft cries of her newborn daughter filling the silence. She gazed at the baby, her heart heavy yet resolute. The door creaked open, and she turned to see Vittal's mother standing there, her face a mask of cold fury.

Without acknowledging the baby, Vittal's mother stepped closer, her posture stiff with contempt. Her voice was low, almost a hiss. "You've made a spectacle of yourself, Satya. Running to the court, dragging our family's name through the mud. Do you think anyone will believe you? Do you think you'll win against us?"

Satya placed her daughter gently in the cradle, her hands steady, her movements deliberate. She turned to face the older woman, her expression calm but firm. "I don't just think it," she said, her voice unwavering. "I know I will."

Vittal's mother scoffed, taking a step closer. "You foolish girl. You're nothing without us. No one will stand by you. You'll be left to rot, humiliated and forgotten. Stop this madness now, or I promise you, you'll regret it."

Satya didn't flinch. She stepped forward, closing the gap between them, her eyes locking onto the older woman's with a fire that burned through the tension in the room.

"Regret?" Satya's voice was steady, cold as steel. "Do you think I don't already know regret? I regret trusting your son. I regret enduring years of abuse in silence. I regret letting fear dictate my life. But there's one thing I don't regret—standing up for myself and my daughter."

The venom in Vittal's mother's eyes faltered for a moment, replaced by uncertainty.

"You've underestimated me," Satya continued, her tone cutting. "You thought I'd stay quiet, that I'd keep enduring your cruelty. But you were wrong. I've lost too much, suffered too deeply to let your threats scare me. I've already been broken, but I've built myself back piece by piece. And this time, I'm unbreakable."

Vittal's mother's lips curled into a sneer, but the slight tremor in her hands betrayed her. "You're just a woman—a weak, insignificant woman. What can you possibly do against us?"

Satya's voice rose, firm and commanding. "You're right about one thing—I am a woman. And that's my greatest strength. I've endured pain you can't even fathom and still found the courage to fight. For every woman you've silenced, for every cruelty you've justified, I'll stand. I'll make sure the court knows the truth, and I'll make sure my daughter never grows up in a world where people like you can thrive unchecked."

The older woman's face twisted with anger, but she took a step back, her footing less sure.

"This is far from over," she spat. "You'll regret crossing us."

Satya took a step closer, her presence commanding. "You should be the one regretting, not me. Regret every slap, every insult, every threat. Regret thinking I'd crumble. Because this is just the beginning. I'll fight you in court, and

I'll fight you in life. You can try to ruin me, but you'll fail. I'm not going back. Not now. Not ever."

As Vittal's mother stormed out of the room, the door slamming behind her, Satya stood tall, her chest rising and falling with the strength of her conviction.

She turned back to her daughter, a quiet determination settling over her. "For you," she whispered, brushing her fingers against the baby's tiny hand. "For both of us. We're free now, and we'll never go back."

ഇ

The night before the court date, the air in my room felt heavy, thick with a mixture of fear and resolve. My daughter lay beside me, her tiny chest rising and falling in the peaceful rhythm of sleep. Her innocence was a stark contrast to the storm raging in my mind. Every possible outcome of tomorrow played out in my head, each one as nerve-wracking as the last. I told myself I had to be strong—for her, for me. But the silence of the night only amplified my doubts.

Suddenly, I heard it—a faint crunch of footsteps outside the window. My body tensed, the sound sending a cold shiver down my spine. My heart pounded in my chest as I turned toward the sound. My breath caught when I saw Vittal's shadowy figure outside, illuminated by the dim glow of the streetlamp. His face was twisted into a snarl, malice etched into every line.

Before I could react, he smashed the window with a swift, brutal motion, glass shards raining down like jagged tears. My daughter stirred beside me but didn't wake. I scrambled to shield her as Vittal climbed through the broken frame, his voice a venomous hiss.

"You think you can take me down, Satya? You think you can ruin my family's name?" he spat, his words dripping with contempt and rage. His eyes were wild, his demeanor more dangerous than I had ever seen.

I tried to scream, but terror clamped down on my throat. My parents rushed into the room, their faces pale with fear, but Vittal's goons followed close behind, blocking their path. My mother cried out, my father struggled against the men holding him back, but their strength was no match.

Tears blurred my vision as I clutched my daughter to my chest, panic coursing through me. Just as Vittal took a menacing step forward, a loud crash came from the door.

Ashrith.

Maggi's brother burst into the room like a force of nature, his broad shoulders filling the doorway. His face was a mask of unrelenting determination, and his voice was a roar. "Get away from her!"

Before anyone could react, Ashrith charged at Vittal and his men. The room erupted into chaos. Fists flew, grunts and cries echoed off the walls. Vittal's men lunged at Ashrith, but he was relentless, his movements swift and calculated. One by one, they fell, groaning in pain.

I held my daughter close, shielding her from the scene, but I couldn't tear my eyes away. Ashrith fought like a man possessed, his strength and resolve unmatched. Vittal, seeing his men subdued, staggered back, his bravado crumbling.

"You'll regret this, Satya!" he screamed, desperation lacing his words as he stumbled toward the window. "This isn't over!" But his threats were hollow, his power stripped away by the sheer force of Ashrith's presence. He fled into the night, his goons limping after him, leaving behind shattered glass and a room charged with tension.

As silence fell, Ashrith turned to me, his chest heaving from exertion. His eyes softened as he spoke, his voice steady and reassuring. “You’re safe now, Satya. We won’t let anyone hurt you or your family again.”

My tears came then, hot and unstoppable. Relief mixed with gratitude as I held my daughter tightly, whispering a silent prayer of thanks.

Maggi arrived moments later, her face pale but her expression determined. She rushed to my side, pulling me into a fierce embrace. “Satya, I’m so sorry. I should have been here sooner. I’ll never let them near you again.”

The gravity of what had just happened settled over me. My fear began to ebb, replaced by a burning resolve. They had tried to intimidate me, to silence me, but they had failed. I wasn’t just a victim anymore—I was a mother, a daughter, a fighter.

XIX

Prevail

The next morning, the sun rose with an unusual brilliance, its golden rays streaming through the curtains as if nature itself was urging me to rise and face the day. I stood by the window, letting the light wash over me, my heart heavy yet resolute. Today would be pivotal—not just for me, but for my daughter and the life we deserved.

Ma entered the room, carrying a cup of milk. "Satya," she said softly, her voice a balm to my nerves. "Drink this. You'll need your strength today."

I took the cup, my hands trembling slightly. "Ma, what if... what if they manage to convince the court? Vittal's family has money, influence..."

She placed a firm hand on my shoulder. "You have something they don't, Satya—truth and the courage to stand up for it. Remember, you're not alone. We're all here with you."

Appa joined us, his expression stoic but his eyes glistening with unspoken pride. "This isn't just your fight, Satya. It's ours. They won't win—not today."

A soft knock at the door interrupted us. Maggi and her husband, Vijay, stood there, flanked by Ashrith. "Are you ready?" Maggi asked, her eyes scanning mine for doubt.

I nodded, setting the cup down. "As ready as I'll ever be."

We walked together, a united front as we headed to the courthouse. My daughter held my hand, her tiny fingers wrapping around mine. Her innocent smile gave me strength. Behind me, my parents and friends formed a fortress of support. I could feel their quiet determination, their belief in me, buoying me forward.

As we approached the courthouse, I spotted Vittal's family at the entrance. Vittal stood in the center, his shoulders squared, his face twisted into a smug expression that made my stomach churn. His parents flanked him, their eyes flickering with a mixture of disdain and confidence. Meena, his sister, stood slightly apart, her lips curled in a smirk.

"They look too sure of themselves," Vijay muttered under his breath. "Typical."

Maggi touched my arm. "Ignore them. Today isn't about their arrogance—it's about your strength."

I exhaled deeply as we entered the courtroom. The atmosphere was thick with anticipation, the hum of whispered conversations punctuated by the shuffle of papers and the clicking of heels. Vittal's lawyer, a man who seemed to thrive on manipulation, was already at his desk, flipping through a stack of documents with an air of smug efficiency.

"Look at him," Ashrith muttered, his voice low with disdain. "Like he owns the place."

The courtroom buzzed with quiet murmurs as I took my seat. My hands trembled slightly, but I held my head high. The judge's gavel would soon decide my fate, but in my heart, I knew I had already won. I had reclaimed my voice, my dignity, and my right to live without fear.

This was no longer just my fight—it was for every woman who had suffered in silence, for every child born into uncertainty, for every person who dared to dream of freedom. Today, I would make my stand.

ℵ

The courtroom was tense as the judge entered, his gavel striking with an authoritative thud. My pulse quickened, but I forced myself to stay calm. The stakes were high—not just for me, but for my daughter, for my family, and for every moment I had endured in silence.

Vittal's lawyer rose first. He was a man who reeked of overconfidence, his slicked-back hair and smug expression perfectly complementing his oily demeanor. His voice carried a practiced smoothness, designed to sow doubt.

"Your Honor," he began, his smirk almost taunting, "the allegations brought forth by Mrs. Satya Sree are nothing but a web of lies and deceit. My client, Vittal, is a man of integrity, wrongfully accused by a woman desperate to tarnish his name." His words hung in the air, calculated to sting.

He produced a stack of documents and placed them before the judge with an exaggerated flourish. "I present evidence to prove that the claims of abuse are fabricated. These hospital records are manipulated, the timelines inconsistent. Furthermore, I have photographic proof that discredits Mrs. Satya Sree's character entirely."

Gasps rippled through the courtroom as a slideshow of doctored photographs appeared on the projector. My heart sank as I saw myself with Karthik, a man from my past. Those moments had been innocent, remnants of a life I had long left behind. But Vittal's lawyer twisted them into a sordid tale.

"Mrs. Satya Sree," he continued, his voice dripping with venom, "Was involved in a relationship with this man, Karthik, even while she was married to Vittal. These messages"—he held up printed screenshots—"prove her infidelity. What kind of mother behaves in such a disgraceful manner?"

Vittal's family, seated smugly to one side, exchanged triumphant glances. They thought they had buried me. But they didn't know me anymore. I wasn't the same woman who had silently endured their cruelty.

I rose to my feet, forcing myself to meet the judge's gaze. "Your Honor, these pictures and messages have been taken completely out of context. The photographs are from a time before I even met Vittal. The messages? They were exchanged with Karthik during a difficult period in my life when he was a friend offering support—not some illicit affair."

Before Vittal's lawyer could interject, Maggi stood. Her presence was a force, her voice unwavering. "Your Honor, I know Satya Sree. I've stood by her through every trial she's faced. Karthik was nothing more than a friend who helped her during a vulnerable time. To use these moments against her is not just deceitful—it's cruel."

The lawyer sneered, clearly frustrated that I hadn't crumbled under his accusations. "Vittal Krishna is a respected man in the community, Your Honor. This is nothing more than an attempt to extort his family's wealth and ruin his reputation."

The judge raised a hand to silence him. "Enough. This court will rely on verified evidence, not conjecture. We will review every document, photograph, and testimony before drawing any conclusions."

Next, the witnesses began to take the stand. Ashrith, Maggi's Brother, was the first. His commanding presence filled the room as he recounted the events of the previous night. His voice was steady, recounting in vivid detail how he had thwarted Vittal's attempt to intimidate and harm me.

"They broke into her home," Ashrith said, his voice cold with controlled anger. "They threatened her, shattered her windows, and tried to silence her. I was there. I saw it with my own eyes. This isn't just about lies in court; this is about a man who thinks he can use fear as a weapon."

Ashrith, a friend and neighbor who had witnessed Vittal's outbursts, also testified. His words painted a picture of the emotional torment I had endured. "Satya isn't lying," he said firmly. "I've seen how Vittal treated her—like she was nothing more than an object to control."

Each testimony felt like a chisel, breaking apart the carefully constructed façade of Vittal's innocence. The atmosphere in the courtroom shifted. The smirks on Vittal's family's faces began to falter, replaced by unease.

As the day drew to a close, the judge addressed me directly. His expression was stern but not unkind. "Mrs. Satya Sree, tomorrow will be critical. Are you prepared for the cross-examination?"

I stood tall, holding my daughter's tiny hand for strength. Her innocent eyes looked up at me, unaware of the storm around us but a reminder of why I couldn't back down.

"I am ready, Your Honor," I said, my voice unwavering. "I will not be A Silenced Woman."

The courtroom buzzed with murmurs as the judge adjourned for the day. As we stepped outside, Maggi placed a reassuring hand on my shoulder. "You were incredible in there, Satya. They threw everything at you, and you didn't flinch."

I took a deep breath, my resolve unshaken. Vittal's family had underestimated me. They thought their lies and manipulations would bury me. But I had truth on my side, and I was ready to fight for it, no matter the cost. Tomorrow, I would face them again—and this time, I would not just survive. I would prevail.

XX

Judgement

The final day of the trial dawned, bringing with it a heavy stillness that seemed to press down on my chest. I stood outside the courthouse, holding my daughter close. Her tiny hand clutched my scarf, grounding me. This wasn't just about me anymore—it was about ensuring her future, free from the shadows of Vittal's cruelty.

Inside, the courtroom buzzed with subdued whispers. Vittal's family sat in a row, their faces masks of feigned innocence. Vittal's lawyer, his smirk sharper than ever, adjusted his papers, preparing for what he clearly thought would be my downfall.

As I took the stand, my heart raced, but I met the judge's gaze with unwavering resolve.

The lawyer rose, his posture exuding arrogance. "Satya Sree," he began, his voice dripping with mockery, "Isn't it true that all of this—this drama—is nothing more than an elaborate act of revenge because your marriage ended?"

I leaned forward, my voice steady and clear. "No, it's not revenge. It's justice. I endured years of cruelty and abuse in silence. Today, I'm here to make sure no one else endures the same."

The lawyer arched an eyebrow, feigning disbelief. "What proof do you have of this so-called abuse?"

I took a deep breath, suppressing the flicker of anger his dismissive tone ignited. "I have proof," I said firmly, "Plenty of it."

Maggi handed me a folder filled with documents. I presented hospital records detailing injuries I had suffered at Vittal's hands. The judge studied them closely. Then came witness statements from neighbors who had heard the shouting, the threats, and had seen me bruised and battered.

The lawyer leaned against the podium, his tone casual but biting. "These could all be coincidences, could they not? A fall here, a misunderstanding there. Surely, this doesn't prove abuse."

I met his gaze, calm but unyielding. "You're right. That's why I have more."

Maggi stepped forward with a tablet. I played a video, the room falling deathly silent as Vittal and Madhu—his mistress—appeared on the screen in a compromising position. Vittal's smug expression crumbled into shock, his family shifting uncomfortably in their seats.

The lawyer jumped to his feet, his face flushed with fury. "This is inadmissible! Where did you get this footage?"

I met the judge's gaze. "Your Honor, the video was obtained from a private investigator. It's legitimate and directly relevant to this case."

The judge nodded, signaling the court clerk to add it to the evidence file.

"And there's more," I continued, pulling up a series of WhatsApp messages between Vittal and Madhu. The texts were explicit, detailing their affair and mocking me for being too "weak" to leave.

The lawyer's voice rose in desperation. "This doesn't prove cruelty! A man's personal indiscretions don't justify these accusations!"

I steadied myself, the tremble in my voice now fueled by emotion. "During my pregnancy, Vittal beat me, calling me worthless. He refused to let me seek medical care, forcing me to suffer in silence. On the day of my labor, he threw me out of the house. My neighbors had to take me to the hospital because my husband—the father of my child—didn't care."

The courtroom was silent, save for the occasional shuffle of papers or whispered gasp.

Mrs.Archana, one of my neighbors, stepped forward to testify. Her voice cracked with emotion. "I remember that day vividly. Satya was in so much pain, and Vittal didn't even flinch as he locked her out. We couldn't bear to watch. We delivered the baby outside the Vittal house and then we took Satya and rushed her to the hospital ourselves."

The judge listened intently, his expression growing more severe as the truth unfolded.

But I wasn't done. Turning to Vittal's family, I faced them directly, my voice unwavering. "Your treatment was just as abusive. You belittled me, called me worthless, and made me feel like I was nothing."

Vittal's mother's face turned a furious shade of red. "That's a lie!" she hissed, but the judge's gavel silenced her outburst.

"Meena," I continued, now addressing Vittal's sister, "You mocked me constantly. My appearance, my cooking, even my ability to raise a child—you tore me down at every opportunity, as if my existence was a joke to you."

Meena's eyes flashed with anger, but she said nothing.

"And then there was you," I said, fixing my gaze on Vittal's father. His face had gone pale, beads of sweat forming on his brow. "You threatened me time and again, telling me that if I left, I'd never see my daughter again. You said I was nothing without your family, that I'd be a disgrace to my parents."

The judge's stern gaze shifted to Vittal's father, who fidgeted under its weight.

The lawyer's composure was unraveling. He shuffled his papers, his arguments faltering. "These are just words—"

"Words that were corroborated by witnesses!" Maggi interrupted, her voice ringing with conviction.

The judge raised a hand for silence. "I've heard enough. We'll reconvene shortly for the verdict."

As I stepped down, I caught a glimpse of Vittal. His once-arrogant smirk was gone, replaced by fear. His family looked equally shaken. They had underestimated me, thought they could silence me with threats and lies. But the truth was louder.

I returned to my seat, my daughter reaching for my hand. Maggi squeezed my shoulder. "You've done it, Satya. You've shown them your strength."

I held my head high, knowing that no matter the verdict, I had won. I had fought for myself, for my daughter, and for every woman who had ever been silenced. This was my moment, and I had reclaimed it entirely.

The courtroom fell silent, the weight of my testimony and evidence hanging heavily in the air. All eyes turned to the judge, who leaned forward, his expression grave and commanding.

The judge's voice broke the silence, sharp and deliberate. "Vittal," he said, his gaze piercing.

"Show me one shred of evidence that you took Satya to the hospital during her pregnancy. Just one piece of proof that you cared for her or her child. If you can provide that, I will dismiss this case immediately."

The air grew electric with tension. Vittal's face turned ashen, beads of sweat forming on his brow. His eyes darted frantically around the room, searching for a lifeline where there was none. He stammered, his voice barely audible. "I... I don't have..."

"Answer me clearly!" the judge's voice thundered. "Did you ever take responsibility for your wife's wellbeing? Did you ever ensure her safety?"

Vittal hung his head, his silence damning. His family shifted uncomfortably in their seats, their earlier smugness replaced by dread.

The judge leaned back, his face stern. "So, I understand. These allegations are not just accusations; they are truths corroborated by evidence and witness testimony. Vittal's family, do you have anything to say in your defence?"

Vittal's father hesitated before standing, his voice trembling. "We... We were only trying to protect our son, Your Honor. To protect our family's reputation."

The judge's eyes narrowed, his tone unrelenting. "Protect? By abusing and torturing your daughter-in-law? By throwing her out of your home while she was in labor? By denying her medical care and dignity? You call that protection?"

The courtroom buzzed with murmurs, the spectators' shock and anger palpable. Vittal's father sat down, his head bowed, unable to meet the judge's gaze.

The judge raised his gavel, his voice cutting through the noise. "Order in the court!"

Silence fell once again, but this time, it was filled with a collective anticipation.

The judge's voice rang out, steady and resolute. "The court finds Vittal guilty of domestic violence, emotional abuse, and adultery. Satya, you are granted full custody of your child. Furthermore, Vittal is ordered to pay compensation for the pain and suffering he has caused."

Relief washed over me, tears streaming down my face as Maggi and my parents rushed to my side, embracing me tightly. The weight of years of torment began to lift, replaced by a sense of triumph and justice.

But the judge wasn't finished.

"Additionally," he continued, his tone as cold and unyielding as steel, "Vittal and his family are found complicit in enabling and perpetuating this abuse. Their actions have caused irreparable harm to Satya Sree and her child. As such, this court sentences Vittal and his family to one year of imprisonment."

Gasps echoed through the courtroom. Vittal's face crumpled in disbelief, his arrogance shattered. His father's face turned beet red with rage, but one stern look from the judge silenced any protests.

"You have shown no remorse, no accountability," the judge declared. "Instead, you sought to silence and intimidate Satya. This court will not tolerate such cruelty. Today, justice is served."

The gavel came down with a resounding crack, sealing their fate.

As the bailiffs approached, Vittal and his family were led away in handcuffs. Vittal glanced back, his expression a mix of anger and desperation, but I met his gaze with unwavering strength. For once, I was no longer afraid.

The murmurs in the courtroom grew louder as the crowd began to disperse, but I remained rooted in place, clutching my daughter close. Maggi leaned in, her voice soft but triumphant. "You did it, Satya Sree. You're free."

My parents held me tightly, their tears mirroring my own. "We're so proud of you," Ma whispered, her voice thick with emotion. "You've shown incredible courage."

I kissed my daughter's forehead, her tiny fingers curling around mine. "We're safe now, my love," I murmured, my heart swelling with a sense of peace I hadn't felt in years. "Our new beginning starts today."

The courtroom slowly emptied, but the moment lingered. I had fought for my dignity, for my freedom, and for my child's future. And against all odds, I had won. As I stepped out into the bright sunlight, I felt the warmth of hope on my face. This wasn't just a victory in court—it was a victory for every woman who had ever been silenced, every mother who had ever been told she was powerless.

I stood tall, my daughter in my arms, ready to embrace the life that lay ahead.

XXI

Societal

As I settled into my new routine, I began to feel the suffocating weight of societal judgment. It was subtle at first—a lingering glance from a neighbor, a hushed conversation that abruptly stopped when I entered the room. But soon, it became impossible to ignore. The whispers grew louder, their edges sharp and cutting.

"She's a divorcee, you know."

"Her character must be questionable."

"She must have done something to deserve it. No woman leaves her husband for no reason."

These words carried more venom than any overt insult. They seeped into every corner of my life, wrapping around me like a shroud of invisible shame.

Even my parents, my unwavering pillars of support, felt the sting of this societal disdain. Ma, who had always spoken her mind, now chose her words carefully in public, her confidence dimmed by the unspoken fear of fueling the gossip. Appa, who had faced countless challenges in life with quiet resilience, now avoided the judgmental eyes of our neighbors.

At home, they tried to shield me, offering solace in the form of Ma's gentle reminders of my strength and Appa's reassuring pats on my shoulder. But I could see the worry in their eyes, the frustration they didn't voice. They bore the burden of my pain in silence, trying to absorb the societal blows that were meant for me.

The isolation grew heavier each day. Every trip outside felt like walking into a courtroom where the world had appointed itself judge and jury. On one particularly bright afternoon, as I stepped out to run errands, I overheard two women standing by the gate.

Two women, Lakshmi and Jayanthi, stood near the gate of a house, their hands busy with the daily chore of picking vegetables from the vendor. Their eyes, however, were trained on Satya, who was walking down the street with her head held high, cradling her baby.

Lakshmi: (smirking, her voice low but sharp) "Look at her, walking around like she owns the place. No mangalsutra, no kumkum on her forehead. What kind of woman does that?"

Jayanthi: (gasping dramatically) "Exactly! She's not even trying to hide it anymore. How shameless can she be? A married woman without her symbols? I tell you, she's practically advertising herself!"

Lakshmi: (nodding conspiratorially) "And with a baby in her arms! Can you imagine the disgrace she's bringing to her family? No wonder her husband isn't around. Poor man, he must be so ashamed."

Jayanthi: (snickering) "Ashamed? I wouldn't blame him if he left her. Women like her... they don't know their place. Always trying to act so bold, so independent. And look where that gets them—alone, and the whole town talking about them."

Lakshmi: (leaning closer, whispering loudly enough for Satya to hear) "Did you hear? She's even taken him to court. Can you believe the nerve? A wife dragging her own husband to court! Who does that?"

Jayanthi: (laughing maliciously) "Oh, I'm sure she has her reasons. Probably wants his money or something. That's what these modern women do—destroy families and play the victim."

Satya stopped in her tracks momentarily, her grip tightening on her baby. She could feel the heat rising in her cheeks, but she forced herself to keep walking. Her head remained high, even as their words struck like daggers.

Lakshmi: (raising her voice, pretending to talk to Jayanthi but ensuring Satya could hear) "You know, I pity her child. Growing up without a father, surrounded by a mother with no shame. What kind of example is that?"

Jayanthi: (clucking her tongue) "Exactly. That poor child is going to grow up with people pointing fingers, whispering behind their back. And all because of a mother who doesn't know how to keep her mouth shut and her family intact."

As Satya walked past them, she turned her head slightly, meeting their eyes with a fierce, unflinching gaze. Her silence was deafening, her dignity an armor they couldn't pierce.

Behind her, the two women faltered for a moment, Lakshmi nervously glancing away.

Lakshmi: (huffing, trying to recover) "See? No shame at all. Just staring like that. Truly, she's lost all respect."

Jayanthi: (less confident, muttering) "Yes... but maybe we shouldn't push too far. She looked... different."

Satya's steps grew stronger, her resolve firmer. Their words no longer had the power to break her. She was done letting their gossip define her life.

Taking a deep breath, I straightened my shoulders and walked past them with deliberate calm, my head held high. My silence was not acceptance—it was defiance. I refused to give them the satisfaction of seeing my pain.

But the encounter stayed with me, lingering like a bruise. That evening, as I sat in the dim light of my room, I found myself questioning everything. Why did my mangalsutra—or the lack of it—matter so much to them? Why was a woman's worth tied so closely to her marital status? And why did society view my choice to leave a toxic marriage as a reflection of my morality?

I thought of my daughter, sleeping peacefully in the next room. The thought of her growing up in a world where women were judged so harshly filled me with dread. I knew then that I couldn't let this break me. I had to show her—and myself—that our worth was not defined by the opinions of others.

ꕥ

The next day, I resolved to start rebuilding my life—not to prove anything to society, but to reclaim my sense of self. I enrolled in an online course to update my skills, something I had always wanted to do but had put off during my marriage.

Ma noticed the change in me. "What are you working on, satya?" she asked one morning, placing a steaming cup of filter coffee beside me.

"I've started a course," I replied, unable to keep the pride out of my voice. "I want to get a better job, Ma. I want to stand on my own feet."

She smiled, her eyes welling up with tears. "That's my girl," she said, cupping my face.

My determination was tested again and again in the weeks that followed. Every step forward felt like swimming upstream against a current of criticism and doubt. But with each small victory—a completed assignment, a positive email from an instructor, a moment of laughter with my daughter—I felt pieces of my shattered confidence knitting themselves back together.

ꕥ

That evening, as I sat on the balcony with a cup of tea, the weariness of the day weighed heavily on me. The murmurs, the sidelong glances, the incessant feeling of being under a microscope—all of it made my chest tighten. My daughter was asleep, and Ma and Appa were in the living room, speaking in hushed tones. I closed my eyes, letting the cool breeze caress my face, but the tension refused to ease.

Just then, my phone buzzed. It was Ashrith..

"Satya," he said, his voice warm but laced with concern. "How are you holding up?"

I hesitated for a moment, considering brushing it off with a simple "I'm fine." But this was Ashrith.—my rock, my confidante. "I don't know, Ashrith.," I admitted, my voice cracking slightly. "It's hard. Everywhere I go, I feel their eyes on me, judging me, dissecting every choice I've made."

Ashrith. sighed. "Of course they're judging you. People love to talk, especially when it's about something they don't understand. But Satya, tell me this—are you living your life for them?"

His question caught me off guard. "No, but it feels like their opinions are everywhere, like I can't escape them. Even Ma and Appa are affected. I see the way they avoid going out too much now. I feel like I've brought shame to them."

"Shame?" Ashrith.'s voice sharpened. "Satya, stop right there. You didn't bring shame to anyone. What you did—leaving a toxic marriage and standing up for yourself—takes courage. Do you have any idea how many women wish they had your strength? How many stay silent because they're too afraid of this exact judgment? You didn't just fight for yourself; you fought for your daughter's future, for your dignity."

His words hit me like a jolt. I opened my mouth to respond but found myself at a loss for words.

"Listen to me," Ashrith continued, his tone softening. "Yes, people will talk. They'll always talk. If you'd stayed in that marriage, they would've whispered about how you were too weak to leave. Now that you've left, they're whispering about how you dared to defy societal norms. Do you see the pattern here? It's not about you, Satya—it's about them needing something to gossip about. You could be perfect in every way, and they'd still find a reason to point fingers."

I leaned back in my chair, his words sinking in. "But Ashrith., it's not just the whispers. It's the way they look at me, like I'm some cautionary tale or, worse, a spectacle. Today, I overheard someone say that because I don't wear a mangalsutra, I must be 'available.' Can you imagine how humiliating that is?"

Ashrith's anger was palpable even over the phone. "What nonsense! And these are the same people who'll preach about morals and values at every festival. Hypocrites, the lot of them. Satya, don't let their small minds dictate your worth. You've done nothing wrong. In fact, you've done everything right by standing up for yourself and refusing to be mistreated. Do you really think their opinions matter in the grand scheme of your life?"

I stayed silent, my fingers gripping the mug in my hands.

"Satya," Ashrith continued, his voice gentle now, "You are so much more than the labels they try to stick on you. Divorcee, single mother, whatever—they're just words. What truly defines you is your resilience, your kindness, your ability to rise even when the world tries to pull you down. And let me tell you something else—you're teaching your daughter the most important lesson of all: that her value doesn't depend on anyone else's approval."

Tears welled up in my eyes, and I didn't bother wiping them away. "I know you're right, Ashrith," I said, my voice trembling. "But it's so hard. Some days, I feel like I'm drowning in it."

"I know it's hard," Ashrith said softly. "But you're not alone. I'm here, maggi's here, and so are your parents. And let me remind you of something: the best way to silence those whispers is to live your life on your own terms. Let your success, your happiness, and your peace speak for you."

"But where do I even start?" I asked, the question heavy with desperation.

"Start with yourself," Ashrith said. "Take small steps. Do things that make you feel proud and happy. Remember that seminar I mentioned? Come with me. You'll meet women who've faced worse and come out stronger. Their stories will inspire you. And you need to see that you're not alone in this."

I hesitated. "I don't know, Ashrith. I'm not sure if I'm ready for that kind of space yet."

"Nonsense," he replied firmly. "You're more than ready. You just don't realize it yet. And if nothing else, do it for your daughter. Show her what it looks like to rise after a storm."

His words hung in the air, filling me with a sense of possibility. For the first time in weeks, I felt a flicker of hope. "Okay," I said finally, a small smile breaking through. "I'll go."

"That's my girl," Ashrith said, his voice bright with pride. "One step at a time, Satya. And remember—you're not defined by your past. You're defined by how you rise from it."

As I ended the call, I felt a strange mixture of exhaustion and exhilaration. Ashrith was right. I couldn't control what people said or thought, but I could control how I chose to live my life. And I was done letting their judgment dictate my story.

The next week, I went to Seminar. I found myself in a room full of women who had stories as powerful as mine. Some had risen from poverty, others had fought against systemic barriers, but all of them radiated resilience.

As I listened to their journeys, I felt a spark reignite within me. Their courage reminded me that I wasn't alone—that I was part of a larger narrative of women who refused to let their circumstances define them.

That day, I left the seminar with a new sense of purpose. The whispers and judgments still followed me, but they began to lose their power. Slowly but surely, I was building a life not of survival, but of meaning and joy. And for the first time in a long while, I felt hopeful about the road ahead.

XXII

New Role

The first day at my new job felt surreal. As I walked through the sleek, glass doors of the office building, a mixture of exhilaration and apprehension bubbled within me. This was a moment I had dreamed of, a milestone that felt like a victory against all odds. My past, my struggles, and the whispers of a judgmental society had not defined me. Today, I was stepping into a new role—not just as a software developer but as a woman reclaiming her narrative.

The open-plan office buzzed with activity: the hum of computers, the soft murmur of conversations, and the occasional burst of laughter. I made my way to the workstation assigned to me, my eyes scanning the unfamiliar faces of my new colleagues. Some offered polite smiles, while others glanced at me with a curiosity that felt almost intrusive. I straightened my shoulders and reminded myself why I was here: not to fit in, but to excel.

The first few weeks were a flurry of introductions, onboarding sessions, and immersing myself in the complexities of the new project. I buried myself in my work, eager to prove my worth through my code and creativity.

Yet, beneath the surface of the professional environment, I sensed an undercurrent of judgment.

It started subtly, almost innocuously—a lingering glance, a curious question about my personal life. "Are you married?" someone asked during a lunch break. When I simply replied, "No," the follow-up—"Oh, so you're single?"—came with a tone that made me bristle.

"No," I said firmly, looking them in the eye, "I'm divorced."

The word hung in the air like a ripple in still water, and I watched as their expression shifted to a mix of surprise and awkwardness. It was as though the very mention of divorce turned me into a puzzle they couldn't resist trying to solve.

The whispers began soon after. I'd catch snippets of conversations that abruptly stopped when I entered the room. "She's divorced, you know..." "Do you think she's—?" I stopped listening, but their words lingered like an unwelcome echo.

80

One afternoon, as I worked intently on debugging a particularly stubborn piece of code, my colleague Harsha approached my desk. He was a confident man, the kind who leaned a little too close when he spoke and laughed a little too loudly at his own jokes. I could sense his presence before he even spoke.

"Hey, Satya," he said, his tone casual, but his posture anything but. He leaned slightly against my desk, his presence invasive, his confidence bordering on arrogance.

I barely looked up, keeping my eyes fixed on the screen. "Hi, Harsha. Need something?"

He chuckled softly, as though amused by my briskness. "Nothing work-related, actually. Just wanted to check in and see how you're settling in. You seem to have fit right in with the team."

"I'm doing fine, thanks," I replied, my fingers continuing to type.

Undeterred, he pressed on. "You know, it's rare to see someone so focused. It's impressive, really. But you must have some time for yourself outside work, right?"

I sensed where this was headed and sighed inwardly. "Harsha, is there something specific you wanted to discuss? I'm kind of in the middle of something here."

He smirked, unfazed by my attempt to cut the conversation short. "Don't be so formal, Satya. I'm just curious. Are you seeing anyone? You don't talk much about your personal life."

I froze for a moment, his audacity taking me by surprise. My hands hovered over the keyboard before I turned to face him fully. "Excuse me?"

"You know," he said, his grin widening, "I was just wondering if you're single. It's no big deal, just making conversation."

The nonchalance in his tone fueled a surge of anger within me. I took a deep breath, steadying myself before responding. "Harsha," I said evenly, locking eyes with him, "my personal life is just that—personal. It's not up for discussion, especially not in the workplace."

His grin faltered slightly, but he quickly recovered. "Hey, relax. I didn't mean to offend you. It's just that, well, people talk. And I thought I'd hear it from you directly."

"People talk," I repeated, my voice laced with incredulity. "And you think that entitles you to pry into my life? Let me make this clear, Harsha: I'm here to work. My personal life is irrelevant to my job, and I'd appreciate it if you respected that boundary."

He shifted uncomfortably, the confident air around him beginning to crack. "Wow, okay. I didn't realize you were so touchy about it. I was just being friendly."

"Friendly?" I said, raising an eyebrow. "There's a difference between being friendly and being inappropriate. What you're doing crosses that line."

The office felt unnaturally quiet as a few heads turned in our direction. Harsha glanced around, clearly uncomfortable with the attention. "Fine," he muttered, his tone defensive. "I didn't mean anything by it. You didn't have to make it a big deal."

"Then don't make it a big deal by asking questions that aren't your business," I replied firmly. "Let's keep our conversations professional from now on."

He muttered something under his breath and walked away, his shoulders stiff. I watched him go, my heart pounding but my resolve unshaken.

As I turned back to my work, I noticed Siri watching from across the room. She gave me a subtle nod of approval, a small smile playing on her lips. It was a moment of solidarity that filled me with quiet strength.

I returned to my screen, my focus sharper than before. For too long, I had allowed others to dictate the narrative, to encroach on my space, and to diminish my worth with their intrusive questions. But not anymore.

This confrontation with Harsha wasn't just about setting boundaries—it was about reclaiming my power. And as I dove back into my code, I felt a newfound sense of confidence. I wasn't just here to work. I was here to thrive.

ഇ

That evening, as I packed up my laptop and prepared to leave, I noticed something that shifted my perspective. A group of women sat in a corner, their faces weary but animated. They were discussing a similar issue—one of them had been asked intrusive questions during a meeting. Another had dealt with inappropriate comments about her attire. Their voices carried a mixture of anger and resignation, but also camaraderie.

I approached them hesitantly, my heart pounding. "Hi," I said, "I couldn't help overhearing. Do you mind if I join you?"

They looked up, their expressions welcoming. One of them, a sharp-eyed woman named Siri, motioned to an empty chair. "Of course. Join us."

As we spoke, I realized that I wasn't alone. These women had faced challenges far greater than mine—judgment, sexism, even outright harassment—but they had survived, even thrived. Their stories were raw and real, but they carried a thread of resilience that inspired me.

"Satya," Siri said, her voice firm, "You have to set boundaries. People will push as far as you let them. Don't be afraid to speak up. You don't owe anyone an explanation for your choices."

Her words stayed with me as I left the office that night. For too long, I had tried to shrink myself, to avoid drawing attention, to blend into the background. But no more. I realized that staying silent was a disservice—not just to myself, but to every woman who had ever been judged, underestimated, or dismissed.

ꕤ

As I walked into the breakroom to grab my morning coffee, I noticed Harsha lounging against the counter, his smirk already in place. He watched me as I approached, his tone as casual as ever.

"Good morning, Satya," he said, his words dripping with familiarity. "Rough night? You look like you've been juggling a soap opera marathon and an all-nighter."

I stopped mid-step, gripping the coffee pot. For a brief moment, I considered ignoring him, but something inside me stirred—a quiet, firm voice that demanded I address this once and for all.

I turned to face him directly, my voice steady. "Harsha, we need to talk."

He raised an eyebrow, his smirk not quite faltering. "Oh? Sounds serious. What's up?"

I kept my tone calm but resolute. "This isn't about me taking things too seriously or lightening up, as you'd like to say. It's about respect. I'm here to work, Harsha, not to entertain your unsolicited comments about my personal life or how I look."

His smirk faded slightly, replaced by a flicker of surprise. "Come on, Satya, I was just joking. No harm intended."

I held my ground, my gaze unflinching. "It doesn't matter what your intention was. What matters is how it feels on the receiving end. Your comments are unprofessional, and they undermine the environment we're supposed to work in. From now on, let's keep our conversations strictly work-related."

Harsha blinked, clearly taken aback. For a moment, I thought he might argue, but instead, he mumbled, "Alright, fine. I didn't mean anything by it, but I'll back off."

I nodded, pouring my coffee. "Thank you. That's all I'm asking for—mutual respect and professionalism. We're all here to do our best, so let's focus on that."

As I turned to leave, I felt a weight lift off my shoulders. Harsha didn't follow me with another remark, and for the first time in weeks, I felt like I had reclaimed a piece of myself in this office.

ꕤ

Later in the Team Meeting

Standing before the team, I presented my ideas with clarity and confidence. My voice didn't waver, and I met every questioning glance with quiet assurance. I wasn't just another employee—they would see me as capable, as someone who belonged.

When I glanced at Harsha during the meeting, I caught him actually listening, a faint look of respect on his face. That was a first.

As I wrapped up my presentation, Siri, seated across the table, gave me a subtle nod and a smile. It was a moment of unspoken solidarity that warmed my heart.

In that room, I wasn't a divorced woman, a subject of gossip, or someone who needed to be pitied. I was Satya—resilient, focused, and unapologetically taking charge of my narrative. I wasn't just surviving anymore. I was thriving, and I was just getting started.

40

XXIII
My legacy

The months that followed my initial confrontation with workplace challenges marked a profound transformation in my life. It wasn't just about settling into a new role—it was about reclaiming my identity, rediscovering my strengths, and realizing the depth of my own potential.

In the bustling ecosystem of our office, my work began to speak for itself. Code reviews turned into lessons for my peers. The once-questioning glances I received morphed into looks of respect and admiration. My contributions were no longer just another set of deliverables—they were benchmarks for quality and creativity.

Every day felt like a small victory, but the real moment of reckoning came 1 year into the job when I received an unexpected email:

Subject: Annual Awards Ceremony - Best Employee Nomination

I stared at the screen, reading and rereading the email. My name, in bold letters, stood beside the category "Best Employee." At first, I thought it was a mistake. Me? The divorced woman who had been whispered about, doubted, judged? But as the reality settled in, I felt an unfamiliar warmth spreading through me—a glimmer of validation, not from society but from the undeniable evidence of my own efforts.

The night of the awards ceremony was filled with excitement and anticipation.The venue glittered with lights, and the air buzzed with anticipation. I sat among my colleagues, trying to blend into the crowd, but the excitement was too infectious.

When the emcee finally announced, "And the Best Employee of the Year award goes to... Satya!" I froze. For a moment, it felt surreal, as though time had stopped. The applause that followed jolted me back, and I rose from my seat, heart pounding, and made my way to the stage.

Standing at the podium, award in hand, I took a deep breath. As I looked out at the sea of faces, something inside me shifted. I spoke—not from a script, but from the heart.

"Thank you," I began, my voice steady yet filled with emotion. "This award is not just a recognition of my professional work; it's a symbol of resilience. For me, it represents the strength to rise after falling, to rebuild after breaking, and to believe in oneself when the world doubts you. To every person here who has faced their own struggles, know this: you are more than the labels society gives you. You are capable of rewriting your story, just as I have started to rewrite mine."

The applause thundered as I returned to my seat, my heart full and my mind alight with possibility.

Winning the award was more than a personal achievement—it was the spark that ignited a long-buried dream. For months, I had been reflecting on my journey, my challenges, and the many women I had met who shared similar struggles. The whispered judgments, the intrusive questions, the silent battles—they weren't mine alone.

The moment I received the Best Employee of the Year award was monumental, but its significance deepened when I carried it home. Clutching the elegant trophy in my hands, I felt its weight—not just as a physical object, but as a culmination of my journey. This wasn't just a symbol of professional excellence; it was the embodiment of resilience, perseverance, and transformation.

ꕥ

When I stepped into my parents' home that evening, they greeted me with warmth and curiosity. My mother's eyes sparkled with pride as she saw the trophy. My father, usually reserved, broke into a rare smile, nodding as though to say, "Well done."

"This is for all of us," I told them, my voice thick with emotion. "For standing by me when the world didn't, for believing in me when I doubted myself."

But as I turned the trophy in my hands, my thoughts drifted to someone else—my daughter, Sakthi. I placed the award gently on the dining table and looked at my parents.

"More than anyone else," I said softly, "This is for her. For my daughter."

My mother's expression softened, her hand finding mine.

"She's watching over you," she said, her voice trembling with emotion. "And she's proud."

I sat with them that evening, sharing the journey behind the award—the challenges, the moments of doubt, and the silent victories. It felt cathartic to acknowledge how far I had come, but the feeling was bittersweet.

Later, in the quiet solitude of my room, I held the hand of my daughter. She has been my greatest source of strength. Her name meant "power," and it was her memory that had kept me going through the darkest days.

"Everything I do is for you," I whispered in her ear while she slept.

That night, as I lay in bed with the soft glow of the award on my bedside table, memories of the past came flooding back. I remembered the cold, empty nights after my divorce, the sting of judgment in every whispered conversation, and the suffocating weight of societal expectations.

I thought of the times I had questioned my worth, doubted my decisions, and felt like the world had collapsed around me. But then I also remembered the small, quiet victories—the day I landed my job, the moment I completed my first project successfully, and the growing confidence that had brought me to this moment.

As tears slipped down my cheeks, they weren't just tears of sorrow. They were a release—a mingling of grief for the woman I once was and pride for the woman I had become.

For the first time, I allowed myself to truly celebrate my achievement. Not just the award, but the journey that had brought me here.

"I did it," I murmured to myself, clutching the hand of my daughter. "We did it."

In the stillness of that night, an idea began to take shape. My story wasn't unique—there were countless women like me, fighting battles that left them silenced. I thought of the women I had encountered, their whispered stories of pain and resilience.

"If I can rise," I thought, "why can't they? And if I can help, why shouldn't I?"

The award, as precious as it was, felt incomplete if it only symbolized my success. It needed to be more—a beacon of hope, a call to action.

As dawn broke, painting the room in soft hues of gold, I made a promise to myself.

I would honor my journey by helping other women rewrite their stories. I would create something meaningful—a platform where women could share their struggles, find their strength, and rise together.

Looking at the trophy one last time before starting my day, I felt a renewed sense of purpose.

"This isn't just for me," I whispered. "This is for every woman who needs to believe in herself again."

And with that thought, Sakthi—the sound of silenced women began to take root in my mind, not just as an idea, but as a mission that would transform lives.

ᘓ

One evening, I shared my thoughts with Maggi and Ashrith over coffee.

"Why don't we create something?" Maggi suggested, her eyes alight with excitement. "A platform where women like us can speak, share, and heal."

Ashrith nodded thoughtfully. "A space where women can find their voice again. It could start small, but who knows how far it could go?"

Their encouragement was the push I needed. Within weeks, Sakthi – The Sound of Silenced Women was born. The name itself was a statement: a declaration that the quiet, suppressed voices of women everywhere deserved to be heard, amplified, and celebrated.

We began Sakthi with modest intentions, starting with small gatherings in rented community halls. At first, it felt uncertain—would women find the courage to come forward? Would they trust this fledgling initiative enough to share their most vulnerable selves? But when the doors opened for our first meeting, any lingering doubts were swept away.

Women from all walks of life trickled in—students eager to build their futures, professionals navigating complex societal pressures, homemakers yearning for recognition, and survivors who carried invisible scars. They came hesitantly at first, but as the room filled, so did the air with a quiet hum of solidarity.

The first woman stood slowly, her hands trembling as she gripped the microphone. Her eyes darted nervously across the room, then lowered to the floor. Her voice wavered, barely audible. "For so long... I thought I was completely alone."

She paused, clutching the mic as though it were the only thing holding her upright. "My husband... he drinks every day. And when he drinks, he becomes... someone else. He doesn't see me as his wife, as a person. To him, I'm just someone to cook for him, clean for him, and bear the brunt of his anger when things don't go his way."

The room fell silent, the weight of her words hanging heavily in the air. She took a shaky breath, her voice breaking. "I stopped hoping a long time ago. Every day, I wake up fearing what mood he'll be in. Every night, I go to bed praying he won't come home drunk. I've lost count of the bruises, the broken things in the house... and in me."

Her fingers tightened around the mic, her knuckles white. "But being here... seeing all of you... it's like a tiny light in a room I thought would stay dark forever."

She lifted her eyes, her gaze meeting the audience for the first time. "Maybe... maybe I don't have to live like this.

Maybe there's a way out. Seeing all of you standing together... it gives me hope that I'm not as powerless as I feel."

Her voice grew firmer, a small but undeniable strength rising within her. "I'm tired of being treated like I'm nothing. And I know now—I'm not nothing. I'm not just a worker in my own home. I'm a person, and I deserve better. We all do."

The room erupted into soft murmurs of support, a few tears falling quietly from the listeners. She took a deep breath, straightened her back, and whispered into the mic, "Thank you for showing me that I'm not alone."

The room erupted in applause, not out of pity but as a collective cheer—a signal that she wasn't alone anymore. That moment felt electric, as if the barriers of silence and shame were shattering, one story at a time.

The session turned into a cascade of shared experiences. Pain and despair intertwined with courage and hope. By the end of the evening, there wasn't a dry eye in the room. But instead of heaviness, the air buzzed with a renewed sense of purpose.

ঌ

What began as monthly meetups soon grew into something far bigger than I had ever envisioned. Maggi, with her infectious energy and connections, reached out to experts and volunteers. Ashrith, a master organizer, streamlined our efforts into something sustainable. Together, we began hosting workshops, seminars, and support groups that addressed the core struggles women faced.

Sessions on financial independence were particularly transformative. Women learned not just how to budget or save but how to negotiate salaries, invest smartly, and build wealth. Mental health workshops created safe spaces to discuss struggles often dismissed in a culture of silence. Self-defense classes taught them not just physical skills but how to reclaim their confidence. And leadership seminars empowered women to take charge—not just in their workplaces but in their lives.

Soon, we launched an online platform. It wasn't just a website—it was a lifeline. Women could connect anonymously, share resources, and find support without fear of judgment. Through this, Sakthi's reach grew exponentially, transcending geographical barriers. Stories poured in from across the country: whispers that turned into roars.

One of our most powerful events was a seminar we titled "Breaking Chains: From Survival to Empowerment." Women who had faced unimaginable odds took to the stage, sharing their journeys. One speaker, a domestic abuse survivor turned entrepreneur, spoke of how she used her pain to fuel her passion. Another, a young girl who had battled societal stigma after leaving an arranged marriage, shared how education became her anchor.

As I listened, I realized how deeply connected we were—not by our struggles alone but by our determination to rise. The room felt alive with energy, a collective resilience that was almost palpable.

Running Sakthi changed me in ways I couldn't have imagined. My identity expanded beyond the confines of my career. I wasn't just a software developer or even a divorced woman reclaiming her life—I was a change-maker, a leader, and a mentor.

Each story I heard became a part of me, reinforcing my belief in the transformative power of our voices. These women weren't just surviving—they were thriving, inspiring others to do the same.

ꕤ

One day, during a workshop on overcoming toxic environments, a young girl approached me. She was barely out of her teens, her eyes wide with a mixture of hope and fear. She clutched a notebook tightly to her chest, as though it contained her entire world.

"Satya ma'am," she began hesitantly, her voice so soft it was almost swallowed by the room's quiet buzz. Her hands were clasped tightly together, and her eyes shimmered with unshed tears. "I just... I just wanted to thank you."

Satya turned her full attention to the young woman, her warm smile encouraging her to continue.

The woman took a shaky breath and spoke again, her words carrying a raw vulnerability. "Listening to you the other day... it was like you were speaking directly to me. You made me realize things I had buried deep, things I was too afraid to face."

She paused, her fingers nervously twisting together. "I was trapped in a marriage that drained me every single day. It was toxic—full of control, anger, and pain. But I stayed because I thought I had no choice. I thought that was my life, that I had to endure it because... because I didn't matter."

Her voice broke slightly, but she pressed on, her words gathering strength. "But when you shared your story, I saw myself in your struggles. And I saw the strength you found to break free. For the first time, I realized I wasn't alone. And I realized... if you could do it, maybe I could too."

A tear slipped down her cheek, but she didn't wipe it away. "I went home that night and packed a bag. I told him I was leaving, and for the first time, I didn't let his threats or anger stop me. I walked out of that house and into a future I'm still scared of—but for the first time in years, I feel free. I feel like I can breathe again."

She looked directly at Satya, her eyes filled with gratitude. "You've changed my life. I don't think I would've had the courage without you. Thank you for reminding me that I matter, that my happiness and dignity matter. Thank you for being the light that showed me the way out of the darkness."

The room was silent, the weight of her words sinking deep into everyone's hearts. Satya reached out and gently touched the young woman's hand, her own eyes glistening with emotion. "You found that strength within yourself," Satya said softly. "I'm so proud of you."

The woman nodded, a small, tentative smile breaking through her tears. It was the smile of someone who had survived, who had finally found hope.

Her words hit me like a wave, leaving me momentarily speechless. I held her hand and replied, "No, my dear. You changed your life. You had the courage to take that first step. I'm just proud to have been a small part of your journey."

That interaction stayed with me long after the event ended. It was a reminder of why Sakthi existed. It wasn't just about me—it was about every woman who dared to rise above her circumstances and find her strength.

ꙮ

The first annual gathering of Sakthi was a turning point. Hundreds of women gathered under one roof, their faces radiating hope and determination. As I stood before them, I felt an overwhelming sense of belonging and fulfillment.

"We are not just survivors," I said, my voice ringing clear across the hall. "We are creators. We are leaders. And together, we are unstoppable."

The applause that followed wasn't just for me—it was for every woman in that room, for the collective strength we had built, and for the revolution we were igniting.

Sakthi was no longer just a platform; it was a movement. It was the sound of silenced women finding their voices, the ripple that would grow into a tidal wave of change.

Looking out at the sea of faces that day, I felt a clarity I had never known before. This was my purpose. Sakthi was my legacy.

XXIV
Award

The years that followed marked an extraordinary transformation, not just for me, but for countless women across the state. Sakthi, the initiative I had founded, blossomed from a small, local gathering of like-minded women into a powerful statewide movement. What began as a humble effort to provide a platform for women to share their stories and demand their rights soon grew into a beacon of hope. It became a symbol of strength, solidarity, and empowerment—a reminder that women, no matter their background, could rise above their circumstances and fight for a better future.

I was no longer just a name on a poster or a figure on a flyer. I became a familiar face in the community—someone who was always at the forefront, advocating for women's rights, equality, and social justice. Everywhere I went, people greeted me with smiles, and I could sense the deep respect they had for the work I had done. My journey had become synonymous with courage and resilience, and I was deeply humbled by the trust that people had placed in me. I knew that none of it had been achieved alone. It had been the collective action of women coming together, sharing their experiences, and standing in solidarity with each other that had made the difference.

Then, one afternoon, as I sat in my office planning the next steps for Sakthi, the phone rang. The voice on the other end was official, calm, and direct. They informed me that I had been selected to receive the state's highest civilian honor for my contributions to women's empowerment. I was stunned. For a moment, time seemed to freeze as the weight of the news settled in. Me, Satya Sree, the woman who had once been silenced, marginalized, and overlooked, was now being recognized as a symbol of hope for women everywhere. The irony was not lost on me. I had spent much of my life fighting against a system that sought to push me into the shadows, and now, that very system was acknowledging the work I had done to dismantle those barriers.

The days leading up to the award ceremony were a whirlwind. I barely had time to process what was happening as my phone rang incessantly with messages of congratulations and well-wishes. I was deeply grateful, but at the same time, I couldn't help but feel a bit overwhelmed. This was no longer just about me—it was about all the women who had walked beside me on this journey, all the women whose struggles and triumphs had shaped the movement we had created.

The day of the ceremony arrived, and I stood before a crowd that seemed impossibly large. My 5 years old daughter, parents, Maggi, Ashrith, and many of the women from the Sakthi community were in attendance. We had come a long way together, and now, this moment was a testament to all that we had accomplished. As I walked to the stage, the applause was deafening. The sound filled my ears, and for a brief moment, I couldn't even hear my own heartbeat. I looked out at the sea of faces, some familiar, some new, all united in their recognition of what we had built. The chief minister, in a formal tone, spoke about my tireless efforts to uplift women, to challenge societal norms, and to pave the way for a future where women could stand tall and speak out without fear.

It was overwhelming. My hands shook as I took the award, but my voice was steady as I began my acceptance speech. I knew what I wanted to say, but when I began to speak, the words came from a place deeper than I had anticipated.

"This award is not just a recognition of my work," I said, my voice carrying across the auditorium. "It is a testament to the power of collective action. It is a reminder that when we come together, we can achieve the impossible. We can move mountains, break down barriers, and change the world."

The room erupted in applause, but I knew in my heart that this moment wasn't truly about me. It was about the thousands of women who had come together, who had found their voices, who had dared to dream of a better world. It was about the women who had fought beside me, who had refused to remain silent. And it was about the next generation of women, who would carry the torch forward, continuing the fight for equality and justice.

As I walked off the stage, the crowd surrounded me, eager to offer congratulations, interviews, and praise. But in that moment, I felt a quiet sense of peace. I wasn't a hero. I was simply a part of a larger movement—a movement powered by the courage and resilience of countless women who refused to accept a life of silence and submission.

The momentum behind Sakthi grew stronger. With every passing year, the movement expanded its reach. We launched new programs to address the specific challenges faced by women in rural areas, in urban slums, and in remote villages. We tackled issues ranging from education to healthcare, from legal rights to economic independence. Sakthi became more than just a campaign; it became a lifeline for women who had nowhere else to turn. Our work touched every corner of the state, and as I looked around, I saw the faces of women who had been empowered to take charge of their lives, who had found strength in the unity we had built.

ઠ૭

Years passed, but the fire within me never dimmed. Looking back now, I realize that my journey wasn't just about one woman's rise—it was about the thousands of untold stories, the struggles, and the victories of women who had long been invisible in society's eyes. It was about the resilience of those women who, despite everything, never gave up on themselves.

The movement had changed the face of our state. A new generation of women was standing up for their rights, challenging the status quo, and demanding a world where equality was not just a distant dream, but a reality. I had gone from being the shy, introverted woman who once feared speaking her truth to becoming the face of a powerful movement for change.

And in the end, what mattered most wasn't the accolades or the awards. It was the lives we had touched, the women who had been inspired to speak out, to rise above their circumstances, and to claim their place in the world. It was about the powerful collective force we had become.

Through Sakthi, we had rewritten the narrative—not just for ourselves, but for future generations. And in doing so, we had created something that could never be taken away: a lasting legacy of hope, strength, and change.

Sakthi became not just a movement but a culture—a culture of empowerment, resilience, and solidarity that spread throughout the state like wildfire. Women from every corner of society, from different walks of life, continued to join our ranks, each with their own stories, struggles, and aspirations. Some had never spoken up before, but through Sakthi, they found their voices. Others, like me, had always dreamed of change but never believed it could be possible. Now, together, we were proving that change was not only possible—it was inevitable.

I continued to lead, not from a place of authority, but from a deep sense of shared responsibility. I knew that my role as a figurehead was not just about being seen—it was about listening, understanding, and reflecting the needs of the women we represented. I worked closely with the Sakthi team, constantly brainstorming new ways to address emerging issues, whether they were economic, legal, or social. We developed programs for vocational training, set up legal aid clinics, and formed alliances with other organizations fighting for women's rights. We created safe spaces for women to share their experiences, and most importantly, we provided a platform for women to become leaders in their own communities.

It wasn't always easy. The road was often riddled with challenges, from bureaucratic red tape to societal resistance. Yet, I had come to learn that the path to true change is rarely smooth. Each obstacle we faced was simply another opportunity to grow stronger, to dig deeper, and to prove that the power of collective action could overcome any adversity.

One of the most poignant moments for me came during a visit to a rural village in the state. The women there, many of whom had never stepped outside their homes without the company of a male relative, were hesitant at first. But after months of outreach and support from our Sakthi teams, they began to gather in small groups, learning about their rights, their health, and how they could contribute to their communities. The first time I spoke to them, I saw the fear in their eyes, the uncertainty of whether their lives could ever change. But by the end of that visit, their faces were different—hopeful, inspired, and eager to begin their own journeys of empowerment.

It was in moments like these that I saw the true impact of our work. This wasn't just about speaking at conferences or receiving accolades. This was about the real, everyday transformations—the quiet victories of women finding the courage to step out into the world and take control of their destinies.

Despite the overwhelming growth and success of Sakthi, there were moments when I questioned my own place in it all. There were times when I felt the weight of responsibility press upon me, when I wondered whether I could keep up with the relentless pace of change. But each time those doubts crept in, I reminded myself of why I had started this journey: not for personal recognition, but for something much greater—the opportunity to rewrite the narrative for women everywhere. I had to remember that the movement wasn't about one person—it was about the power of many, each contributing their unique strength to the collective whole.

Years later, as I stood before a group of young women—many of whom had been born into the very circumstances that I had fought to change—I realized that my work would never truly be "done." It wasn't about reaching a final destination. It was about creating a foundation that would continue to inspire and empower generations to come. The future was theirs now, and I felt a deep sense of peace knowing that Sakthi had planted the seeds of change that would grow into something even more profound in the years ahead.

As I looked at the faces of those young women, eager and bright-eyed, I felt the torch being passed. I saw in them the same determination, the same spark that had driven me all those years ago. And I knew that they, too, would carry the flame forward—passing it on, sharing it, and lighting the way for others. They would be the ones to break through barriers I couldn't even have imagined, to challenge norms I couldn't have dreamed of changing.

The journey had been long, and at times, painful. But it had also been beautiful, transformative, and deeply rewarding. I had gone from being a woman who was silenced, to a woman whose voice could not be ignored. But more than that, I had become a part of something much larger than myself—a movement that was changing the world, one woman at a time.

And in the end, that was what truly mattered. It was never about me or the awards I received or the recognition I gained. It was about the countless women who found their voices, their strength, and their purpose through Sakthi. It was about the stories of resilience, of overcoming insurmountable odds, and of breaking free from the chains of oppression. It was about building a future where women could stand equal to men, where their dreams were just as valid, their voices just as powerful, and their rights just as sacred.

Looking back, I could see it clearly now. Every struggle, every challenge, every setback had been worth it. For in the end, the true measure of success wasn't in the accolades or the recognition—it was in the lives changed, the futures rewritten, and the generations of women who would rise up in the years to come, carrying the message of hope and empowerment that Sakthi had ignited.

And as I stood there, watching the new generation of women take their place in the world, I knew that our movement would never fade. It was a force that would live on, forever shaping the world we had worked so hard to build.

XXV

Silenced

After years of tireless work, I had become accustomed to the constant demands of leading Sakthi. The movement had grown into something bigger than I had ever imagined, spreading across the state and giving women a voice in areas once dominated by silence and oppression. Yet, as the movement flourished, I began to feel the weight of the responsibilities I carried. I had become so immersed in the cause that I had begun to neglect the most important role in my life—being a mother.

My daughter, had always been my rock. She had seen me through my lowest moments, providing support when I felt too exhausted to keep going. I had raised her to be strong, independent, and aware of the world around her. But over time, I realized I had started taking her presence for granted. She had quietly stood by, supporting me in every way possible, but I had missed the signs that she needed me more than ever.

One evening, as we sat together in the warmth of our home, I noticed the quiet sadness in her eyes. She hesitated before speaking, as if unsure whether I would understand or care. “Amma,” she said softly, her voice tinged with vulnerability, “Can we please take a break? Just our family? I want to spend some quality time with you all.”

Her words hit me like a thunderclap. I had been so caught up in the whirlwind of activism and the constant demands of Sakthi that I hadn’t noticed the longing in her voice or the weariness in her heart. I had been giving my all to everyone else, but my own daughter had silently slipped into the background of my life. The realization struck me hard—I had to find a balance. I couldn’t continue to pour everything into a movement without giving the same love and attention to the family that had stood by me through it all.

Without hesitation, I made the difficult decision to step away from the movement, at least for a short time. I knew that I needed to focus on my daughter, on my family, and on recharging my own spirit.

We planned a trip to a quaint, secluded town nestled in the hills—a place where the pace of life was slow, and the air was fresh with the scent of pine and earth. The idea was simple: to escape the noise, to be present with each other in the quiet beauty of nature. We rented a small house at the edge of the town, far from the hustle and bustle of city life, where we could enjoy the peaceful surroundings and reconnect.

The days were blissfully simple. We explored the local markets, tasted fresh fruit from the region, and wandered through the rolling hills, each of us taking time to reflect and enjoy the beauty of the moment. We laughed over homemade meals, shared stories, and let the outside world fade into the distance. For a while, everything felt right. It felt like we were a family again—whole and undistracted by the world’s demands.

But just as I was beginning to relax, to feel the heavy weight of my responsibilities lift, the peacefulness was shattered by the sound of footsteps approaching our little house. At first, it was a faint sound, but then it grew louder, and a sense of unease washed over me. My heart began to race as I looked out the window, but before I could react, a group of men appeared in the doorway, their faces hard and menacing.

My stomach churned. I knew something was wrong.

Among the group, one figure stood out. His eyes were filled with rage, and when he locked eyes with me, the recognition hit me like a punch to the gut. It was Vittal. My ex-husband.

For a moment, I stood frozen in place, my body recoiling as memories of our tumultuous past came rushing back. Vittal had always been volatile, and the animosity between us had festered since our divorce. It was clear from the fire in his eyes that he had come seeking revenge—for what, I didn't know, but the malice in his gaze was unmistakable.

Before I could react, the situation spiraled out of control. Vittal's accomplices, Sampath and Vishwam, barged into the house, overpowering my parents who had accompanied us on this trip. The next few moments unfolded in a blur of chaos. I could hear the sound of fists hitting flesh, the shouts of pain, and the sickening thud of bodies hitting the ground. I screamed, but the sound was swallowed by the violence unfolding before me.

In the midst of the chaos, I watched in horror as my parents were attacked, helpless to do anything. The rage that had been building in me, the years of bitterness and hatred from the past, surged forward, but I was powerless against their cruelty. They were brutally beaten, their lives extinguished before my very eyes.

My heart shattered into a million pieces as I turned to my daughter, who had been standing beside me, her face pale with fear. Her innocent eyes met mine, wide with terror. And then, in an instant, she collapsed to the floor, unconscious.

I tried to reach her, to protect her, but the terror around me was too overwhelming. Vittal and his men were relentless, and the violence in the air was suffocating. As I crouched beside my daughter's motionless form, I realized with a chilling clarity that I had to fight back—not just for myself, but for my daughter, for my family, and for everything I had ever fought for.

In a surge of adrenaline, I gathered every ounce of strength I had left. The pain, the fear, and the sorrow faded into the background as I focused on one singular goal: survival. I wasn't going to let them take everything from me—not again. Not after all that I had fought for.

I launched myself at Vittal, striking out with everything I had. My fists connected with his face, with his chest, but he was stronger—larger—more menacing. He grabbed my arms, trying to twist them behind my back, but I refused to give in. The thought of my daughter, of her safety, pushed me forward. My body burned with anger and desperation, and I found strength I didn't know I had.

The pain was excruciating. Each second felt like an eternity as I struggled to break free from Vittal's merciless grip. Sampath and Vishwam were closing in, their menacing eyes gleaming with dark intent. Every inch of me screamed to fight back, but their sheer force was overwhelming. My body, already battered, had no more strength to give, and yet, I fought with everything inside me.

In a desperate attempt to defend myself, I kicked out at Sampath, my foot connecting with his chest. He grimaced, but his reaction was quick. He grabbed my leg with brutal force and twisted it, causing a sharp pain to shoot up my spine. My breath hitched in my throat, but I didn't stop. I couldn't stop.

Vishwam took advantage of my moment of weakness, pouncing on me with a sickening speed. He pinned me to the ground, the weight of his body pressing down on me, leaving me gasping for air. I could barely move, my limbs crushed beneath him.

Above me, Vittal's cold gaze burned into me. His face twisted in a cruel smile as he looked down on me, savoring my fear. "You think you're so clever, don't you?" he sneered. "You think you can just walk away from me and start a new life? Well, I've got news for you, Satya. You'll never escape me. Not now, not ever."

His words, laced with venom, echoed in my ears, but I refused to let them break me. I had fought too hard for this moment, too hard for the women who had placed their trust in me. I wasn't going to let him take that from me—not without a fight.

With a malicious grin, Vittal pulled a knife from his side. The blade caught the dim light, flashing dangerously before my eyes. I could hear the sickening scrape of the metal as he raised it above me, his eyes glinting with twisted satisfaction. My heart pounded in my chest, and though fear surged through me, I didn't look away.

Sampath and Vishwam held me down with unrelenting force, their grip like iron shackles. There was nowhere to run, no escape. But even as the knife descended, I refused to submit. I had fought for so long, for so many, and this was not where my story would end.

In the moments before the blade could strike, memories flashed before my eyes—of my daughter, my parents, of all the women whose lives had been transformed by the movement I had helped build. I had fought for them, and I would die fighting, but they would carry on the work we had started.

With a surge of adrenaline, I forced the words out, my voice barely a whisper but filled with defiance. "You may kill me," I spat, "but you'll never silence me. My voice will live on. It will haunt you for the rest of your life."

Vittal's face twisted in rage, his fury unleashing in a violent outburst. With a final, brutal motion, he plunged the knife into my neck.

The pain was immediate and overwhelming. It felt as if the world was collapsing around me, and I could feel the warmth of my own blood seeping from the wound. My vision blurred, and my breath became shallow as darkness closed in. But even as my life slipped away, I held on to the one truth I knew in my heart—I had fought with everything I had.

The room spun as the pain from the knife radiated through my body, stealing my strength with every passing second. I could hear Vittal laughing, his cruel, victorious laugh reverberating in my ears like a taunt. My limbs feel heavy, my vision dimming as the world around me blurred into a haze of shadow and light. But even as my body began to falter, my spirit refused to yield.

I looked at my daughter, still crumpled on the floor, her face pale but her chest rising and falling in shallow breaths. Relief coursed through me—she was alive. My parents' motionless forms lay nearby, and a pang of despair gripped my heart, but there was no time to mourn.

This was my end. I could feel it. But it wasn't defeat.

As my knees buckled and I fell to the floor, my eyes met Vittal's once more. His smirk was triumphant, but I saw something else beneath it—fear. He had taken my life, but he couldn't take my legacy. He couldn't take Sakthi's strength, the movement we had built, or the countless voices that would rise because of what we had started.

"You think you've won," I rasped, blood trickling from my lips. My voice was barely audible, but I knew he heard me. "But you haven't. You're a coward, Vittal. A coward who couldn't silence a woman even in death."

His smirk faltered, and for a fleeting moment, doubt flickered in his eyes. I clung to that, to the knowledge that even in my final moments, I had shaken him.

Darkness began to close in, and the sounds of the room faded into a distant hum. My body grew lighter, as if the weight of everything I had carried was finally lifting. My breathing slowed, and the pain receded, replaced by a strange sense of peace.

I thought of my daughter, my hope, my reason for everything. Her name was my final thought, her face the last image I saw as I drifted into the abyss.

And then, there was silence.

EPILOGUE

In the weeks that followed, the news of my death spread like wildfire. The brutal attack sparked outrage across the state, igniting protests and demands for justice. The name Satya became a rallying cry for women everywhere—a symbol of resilience, courage, and the unrelenting fight for freedom.

At my funeral, women from every walk of life gathered, their voices united in sorrow and resolve. They lit candles, sang songs of resistance, and shared stories of how Satya had touched their lives.

Though my body lay at rest, my spirit lived on in every woman who dared to rise, every voice that broke the silence, and every life that found strength in the face of adversity.

I had died fighting, but my death wasn't an end. It was the beginning of a revolution.

ജ

Fifteen years had passed since that fateful night—a night that shattered a family but forged an unbreakable legacy. The seeds planted in my life had grown into a nationwide revolution. Sakthi, the movement had transcended borders and boundaries, becoming a beacon of hope for millions of women fighting for their rightful place in society.

On a crisp winter morning, under a vast azure sky, a stadium unlike any other brimmed with life. Women of all ages, clad in vibrant hues, filled every corner, their voices blending into a hum of anticipation. The air was electric, the atmosphere charged with a mix of reverence and excitement. The sea of women stretched as far as the eye could see—a staggering ten lakh strong, each one a living embodiment of the change we had fought to create.

The stage at the heart of the arena was a masterpiece—a grand platform adorned with banners bearing messages of empowerment, resilience, and hope. At its center, a single microphone stood, waiting for the woman who would soon address the nation.

As the clock struck the hour, the murmurs subsided, and a hushed silence fell over the crowd. Then came the sound of footsteps—deliberate, steady, confident. The collective gaze of the audience turned to the woman emerging from the shadows, her silhouette growing sharper with each step.

There she was—Sakthi Sree.

The applause began as a ripple, spreading like wildfire until the stadium thundered with a deafening roar. Sakthi Sree walked with a poise that commanded respect, her shoulders squared, her head held high. She wore a saree in deep crimson, symbolizing both the sacrifices made and the strength reborn. Her eyes gleamed with determination, her presence exuding an aura that silenced doubt and inspired courage.

Reaching the center of the stage, she paused, taking a moment to soak in the magnitude of what lay before her. She adjusted the microphone to her height and scanned the audience—women from villages and cities, survivors and fighters, dreamers and doers. Each face reflected her own journey: one of struggle, resilience, and triumph.

"My name is Sakthi sree," she began, her voice unwavering yet brimming with emotion. The stadium erupted once again, a thunderous wave of cheers and applause that echoed for miles. She waited, allowing the moment to breathe, before continuing.

"And I am the daughter of Satya sree."

The applause intensified, tears glistening in the eyes of many. Some clutched banners bearing my name, others held photographs of the countless women who had been transformed by the movement. Sakthi Sree took a deep breath, her voice steady as she spoke.

"Fifteen years ago, a woman gave her life so others could find their voices. That woman was my mother—a warrior, a leader, and above all, a believer in the unyielding strength of women. She may no longer be with us, but her spirit lives on in each of us gathered here today."

Her words hung in the air, weaving an invisible thread that connected every soul in the stadium. Sakthi's gaze swept across the crowd, her expression a blend of grief and gratitude.

"My mother taught me that silence is never the answer. That our stories—no matter how painful or messy—are our power. Today, I stand before you, not just as her daughter, but as a woman who has carried her torch, lighting the way for others. And I promise you, I will carry it until my last breath."

The audience was spellbound, their hearts swelling with pride and purpose. As Sakthi spoke, she recounted the journey of the movement—its humble beginnings, the challenges faced, and the triumphs that had paved the way for this historic gathering.

"This is more than a movement," Sakthi declared, her voice rising with conviction. "This is a revolution—a revolution led by women, for women. Together, we have dismantled walls of prejudice, shattered ceilings of oppression, and forged paths of empowerment. And yet, our work is far from over."

Her voice softened, yet it carried the weight of an unshakable resolve.

"We stand here today as proof that change is not a dream. It is a reality we create with our hands, our voices, and our hearts. We are the daughters of Satya Sree, and we will not rest until every woman—every girl—walks this earth with dignity, respect, and freedom."

The applause that followed was not merely loud—it was earth-shattering. Women stood, fists raised, tears streaming down their faces as they cheered for the woman who had become the symbol of their fight.

In that moment, Sakthi Sree raised her hand to calm the crowd. She leaned forward, her voice gentle yet firm.

"I am not just here to lead. I am here to remind you that each of you is a leader. Each of you carries within you the strength to transform this world. Together, we are unstoppable."

From the front rows to the farthest corners, the crowd erupted into chants of "Satya lives on!" The chant grew louder, reverberating across the stadium and into the world beyond.

Sakthi Sree stepped back from the microphone, her face radiant with a sense of fulfillment. Behind her, the massive screen displayed an image of me, her mother Satya sree—a reminder of where it all began.

As the chants grew louder, Sakthi Sree stood tall, the daughter of a dreamer who had dared to believe in change. Her mother's vision was now a reality, and her own legacy was just beginning.

The fire of Satya Sree burned brighter than ever, lighting the way for generations to come.

To be continued.........

An Unsilenced Woman

AUTHOR

Surya Venkatesh
Author | Life Skills Trainer | Motivator | Counselor | Anchor | Dancer

Surya, a multifaceted individual, was born and raised in the picturesque town of **Tanuku**, nestled near the serene River Godavari in Andhra Pradesh. Growing up amidst the natural beauty and vibrant culture of this region shaped his creativity and zest for life. Later, he moved to **Hyderabad**, where he continues to pursue his dreams with unwavering dedication.

A firm believer in the values of faith, god and family, Surya considers these pillars to be his greatest sources of strength and inspiration. When not immersed in his professional endeavors, he enjoys spending quality time with his loved ones, indulging in his love for reading, or exploring cinematic masterpieces that fuel his imagination.

Professionally, Surya is the Head of Soft Skills and Training at the esteemed Wisewings Company, a role that reflects his passion for nurturing potential and empowering individuals. As a seasoned **Soft Skills Trainer, Motivational Speaker, Counselor, and Anchor**, he has made a profound impact by training over 30000 students and 5000 teachers throughout his illustrious career. Surya's motivational workshops and speeches have inspired countless individuals, helping them unlock their potential and embrace a brighter future.

Surya's counseling skills further set him apart. With a compassionate and empathetic approach, he has counseled numerous students and individuals, guiding them through their challenges and helping them move forward in life with confidence and clarity.

From an early age, Surya's talent for dance stood out. What began as a childhood hobby blossomed into a lifelong passion, leading to numerous stage performances and accolades. Among his proudest achievements is being recognized as the **Best Dance Performer** at a **national event**—a testament to his dedication and artistry.

Adding another feather to his cap, Surya has ventured into the world of writing. His debut novel, '**Everything for U**,' is a poignant story that reflects his deep understanding of human emotions and resilience. Following this, he penned his second novel, '**A Silenced Woman**,' a gripping tale that delves into the struggles and triumphs of a woman finding her voice against all odds. Writing has always been a heartfelt passion for him, and his novels are a testament to his ability to touch readers' hearts.

Surya's journey is one of passion, perseverance, and purpose. Whether on stage, in a classroom, or through the pages of a book, he strives to leave a lasting impact, inspiring others to embrace their own unique paths with confidence and courage.

Surya venkatesh

www.ingramcontent.com/pod-product-compliance
Lightning Source LLC
La Vergne TN
LVHW041211150826
845673LV00001B/358

9798897241781